By the tenth ring Erin realized no one was going to answer. A hard, heavy sensation lodged in her stomach. "No one's home," she said.

"Had your parents planned to go out?"

"No." Erin's voice had become a whisper. She hung up the phone. "Something's wrong, Ms. Thornton."

Ms. Thornton put her arm around Erin's shoulder: "Let's not jump to any conclusions. There're lots of possible explanations—" She was interrupted by the sound of someone banging on the back door.

The three of them ran toward it, but Travis got there first and yanked on the handle. A blast of wind and rain blew in with a short, plump woman.

Erin blinked. "Inez!" she cried, recognizing her mother's sales assistant from the boutique. "What are you doing here?"

Inez wrung her hands and grabbed Erin by the forearms. She was crying. "Erin, there's been an accident."

"Mom and Dad?" Erin almost gagged.

"They're at County's emergency room. It's Amy, Erin. Amy's been in a terrible wreck."

Other Starfire Books you will enjoy

BABY ALICIA IS DYING by Lurlene McDaniel

MOURNING SONG by Lurlene McDaniel

A TIME TO DIE by Lurlene McDaniel

MOTHER, HELP ME LIVE by Lurlene McDaniel

LET HIM LIVE by Lurlene McDaniel

SOMEONE DIES, SOMEONE LIVES by Lurlene McDaniel

THE YEAR WITHOUT MICHAEL by Susan Beth Pfeffer

A FAMILY APART by Joan Lowery Nixon

SOMEWHERE BETWEEN LIFE AND DEATH

Lurlene McDaniel

BANTAM BOOKS
NEW YORK • TORONTO • LONDON • SYDNEY • AUCKLAND

RL 5, age 10 and up

SOMEWHERE BETWEEN LIFE AND DEATH
A Bantam Book / January 1991

ISBN 0-553-28349-9

Published simultaneously in the United States and Canada

Bantam Books are published by Bantam Books, a division of Bantam Doubleday Dell Publishing Group, Inc. Its trademark, consisting of the words "Bantam Books" and the portrayal of a rooster, is Registered in U.S. Patent and Trademark Office and in other countries. Marca Registrada. Bantam Books, 1540 Broadway, New York, New York 10036.

PRINTED IN THE UNITED STATES OF AMERICA

OPM 14 13 12 11

This book is dedicated to the memory of Kaitlyn Arquette, September 18, 1970–July 17, 1989—a flower whose season was all too brief—and to her family, who will treasure her memory forever.

I would like to express my thanks to Erlanger Medical Center, Chattanooga, Tennessee, and to Dr. Reggie McLelland of Covenant College.

To every thing there is a season, and a time to every purpose under heaven: A time to be born, and a time to die . . .

—Ecclesiastes 3:1–2 (KJV)

Chapter One

"Where's Amy?"

"Late. As usual." Erin Bennett didn't even try to hide her annoyance.

Her best friend, Shara Perez, heaved a sigh and sprawled across a bench in the deserted studio. "Honestly, Erin, your sister's gonna be late to her own funeral."

"Not so," Erin muttered, adjusting her leotard and stretching her right leg over her head. "*I'll* be in charge of taking her to her funeral, so I know she'll be on time for that."

Shara giggled. "Now what do you suppose Freud would say about that? Maybe you really wish you were an only child, like me."

Erin rolled her eyes, hating to admit that she'd often wished that very thing. And with only fifteen months between her and her sister, Erin realized that she'd never had the luxury of being the one-and-only. "I just think Amy's being a pain," she said. "She knows how much this dance number means to me."

"Come on, Erin. You know Amy's not like that. She never forgets anything on *purpose*."

Erin began to pirouette across the polished dance

floor in wide, sweeping circles. She forced herself to concentrate on her form instead of her anger toward her kid sister. She'd have thought that being a sophomore at Briarwood School for Young Women this year would have matured Amy. Instead, Erin found herself constantly making excuses for her, covering for her tardiness and irresponsible attitude. It was embarrassing, but Erin couldn't seem to stop. Amy always managed to rope her in and get her own way, while still being sweet, outgoing, and likable.

As a junior and the president of the Terpsicord Dance Troupe at Briarwood, Erin felt she had a reputation to maintain among her peers. Amy's lack of seriousness really annoyed her, but she didn't know what to do about it.

The door to the dance studio flew open. "Am I late?" Amy called as she skidded across the oak floor.

Erin stopped spinning, caught her breath, and walked over to where Amy stood, all big blue-eyed innocence. "Three-fifteen, Amy. I said 'Be here by three-fifteen because we have to knock off by four today.' Shara made it on time. I made it on time. But you? Well, as usual we're both standing around waiting for Amy. And you're so late that we're not going to get any serious rehearsing done today. The recital's in March—only four weeks from now." Erin knew she was wasting valuable time, but she was determined not to let Amy off too easily.

"Only four weeks? Yikes! Time's slipping by all right, but just wait till you see what I've got."

"This had better be good, Amy. Ms. Thornton is

counting on the three of us to make this number the high point of the show. I'm beginning to wish I'd never asked you to do the dramatic readings."

"Oh, come on. When I'm a famous actress, you'll look back on this and laugh. Here, take a look at this." She handed Erin a large leather-bound book. "Won't it be perfect on the podium for me to read from? I won't have to use that dorky library book. I can just tuck copies of the readings inside. It'll look so much more elegant, don't you think?"

Erin eyed the old leather-embossed volume, struggling inwardly to stay angry. She had to admit that Amy was right. The book would be so much nicer and would really contribute to the overall effect. "Where'd you get it?"

"It's Travis's grandmother's."

Travis. The name alone made Erin's pulse skip a beat. "Did he loan it to you just for the recital?" She stroked the rich leather cover imagining that Travis had held it.

"Sure."

Erin felt her resolve weakening. Her sister was irrepressible, and no one could stay mad at her for long. That's probably why she attracted friends so easily—as well as the undivided attention of Berkshire Prep's cutest senior, Travis Sinclair.

"It's a nice touch," Erin admitted. Amy grinned and bobbed on the balls of her feet. "But I really need you to be on time," she added sternly, not wanting Amy to think she was off the hook entirely.

"So what are we waiting for? Let's get started."

Erin signaled Shara, who started the music on a cassette player and began to sing. Soon she was immersed in the dance, and once she was lost in her art, nothing else existed. Not even her aggravation with Amy.

"Erin! Come help me get dinner on the table," Mrs. Bennett called.

Erin wandered into the kitchen. "I thought it was Amy's turn to help with dinner tonight," she said. "Where is Amy, anyway?"

"She's working on a history paper that's due tomorrow, and I'm running behind." Her mother rattled pots and pans. "Honestly, I don't know why I ever thought owning my own boutique was a good idea. Customers are so scarce that I should just shut down the place until spring comes."

"Doing a paper! What about *my* homework?"

"Your father and I have the faculty party tonight at Briarwood. I didn't think I'd *ever* get out of the store. Thank goodness Inez could stay until nine and close the place up." She paused from her task of measuring water for rice and pinned Erin with a glance. "You *are* working this Saturday, aren't you? I'm counting on you to hold the fort all day since neither Inez nor I can come in."

Erin almost exploded. "But it's Amy's turn to work. I promised Ms. Thornton I'd help the freshmen dancers for the Terpsicord recital. And speaking of the dance recital, Amy was late again today for our rehearsal. We're never going to get it together for the show if she can't show up on time for practices."

"You've got plenty of time before the show," Mrs. Bennett said. "Besides, I think I gave Amy permission to go do something with the Drama Club on Saturday. Some car wash, I think."

"But it's her turn to work! Just like it's her turn to do dinner."

"Amy's filled in for you plenty of times, Erin. All last week in fact, while you took those extra dance classes."

"But I traded with her two weeks ago so that I'd have last week free."

"Erin, I really don't have time to quibble over how you and Amy keep scorecards over chores. I need help *now*. You know how your father hates to be late. And don't forget, if he wasn't on the faculty at Briarwood, we'd never be able to afford to send you girls there."

Erin held her breath and counted to ten. She didn't have to be reminded that she wasn't in the same league as the rest of the school body, which included Tampa's richest and most socially elite families. Nor was it easy having her sister *and* father at the same school with her. Erin was grateful that he taught computer science, which wasn't a part of her liberal-arts curriculum, so their paths had never crossed in the classroom. Perhaps that was another reason why Amy irked her. It never seemed to bother *her* that they were different from the other girls.

"Erin?" Mrs. Bennett said. "Are you going to stand there staring into space all evening?"

Erin started. "All right, I'll help tonight," she grumbled. "But it really *is* Amy's turn, and I swear this is the last time I get roped into doing *her* chores. You let Amy get away with murder."

"Don't be so dramatic." Mrs. Bennett paused from chopping vegetables. "You know how it is with Amy. Sometimes it seems as if we let her get away with too much; but Erin, you've always been the dependable one. I can always count on you."

"Thanks," Erin muttered, not feeling at all as if she'd been complimented.

Later, sitting at the dinner table, Amy entertained them all with stories about her day at school, and Erin found it impossible to stay mad. Amy *did* have a dramatic streak, and she smiled at Amy's accurate imitation of Miss Hutton's high-pitched nasal voice. "'Miss Bennett,'" Amy mimicked, telling a story on herself. "'If we are going to read Edna St. Vincent Millay aloud, it would behoove us to have read her poetry silently first, now wouldn't it?'"

Mr. Bennett chuckled deeply. "That's exactly how she sounds at faculty meetings too."

"You two are awful," Mrs. Bennett said. "She's just a lonely woman whose whole life is wrapped up in that school and you kids."

"She does donate a lot of her time to charity work," Amy said. "And I'm not knocking her; I just think she's funny."

Erin half listened to the rest of the dinner conversation. She wished she could make her parents laugh the way Amy could. Why couldn't she be less serious about school, her dancing, her whole life? Why did she always feel so out of sync? She looked across the table at Amy. How could two such different people come from the same family? How could two such different individuals coexist in the same house until the day Erin would leave for college?

Erin began to count the days until she would be on her own and free of her pain-in-the-neck, easygoing sister, Amy.

Chapter Two

Later, when their parents had gone out and Erin was alone in her bedroom doing homework, Amy knocked on her door. "I'm busy," Erin announced.

"But I'm lonely."

"How can you be lonely with your radio going full blast? And didn't you just get off the phone?"

Amy cracked open the door and poked her head inside. "I had to tell Travis you were driving me in tomorrow for that—ugh—seven A.M. rehearsal."

"Don't you dare complain! If you were on time for afternoon rehearsals, this one wouldn't be necessary."

Amy stepped into Erin's room. "Don't gripe at me."

"Do you know I work out every morning before school starts?" Erin put her hands on her hips and stood in Amy's path. "Just think, I've stretched and danced for an hour before you even get to your homeroom."

"That's why you're a dancer and I'm into acting. Plays happen at night. Then you go home and sleep until noon."

Erin felt exasperated enough to shake Amy. "You're impossible. Now would you please leave? Unlike some people, I didn't get my work done earlier."

"Are you still mad about that?"

"And about working at the boutique Saturday—"

"Half a day," Amy interrupted. "That's all I'm asking, just one teensy, weensy half a day. The afternoon half. I'll do the morning because I know you're supposed to help Ms. Thornton—"

"No way," Erin was adamant.

Amy dropped dramatically to her knees and clasped her hands. "Oh please, *please*? I'll be your best friend."

Erin stepped around her, out the door, and headed down the hall. "Buzz off. I won't do it."

Amy started after her on her knees, her arms pumping at her sides. Erin refused to watch, because Amy looked so ridiculous, she was afraid she'd laugh and give in to her. "I mean it, Amy, leave me alone." Erin ducked inside Amy's bedroom to escape and stopped short.

Amy almost rammed into the back of her. "What's the matter?"

"Good grief, Amy. It looks like a survival camp in here." Erin stared in dismay at the upheaval. The bed was unmade, clothes hung from chairs and half-open drawers, even the bedside lamp. Papers and books were scattered about the floor.

"My goodness," Amy said mildly. "Maybe thieves broke in."

"How can you *live* like this?"

Amy flounced on her bed, sending pillows and clothes flying. "One of us is neat and orderly, and one of us isn't." She smiled innocently.

"It's nothing to brag about, you know."

Amy jumped off the bed and hauled Erin next to her in front of the mirror. "Look at us, Erin. You're tall, blond, and graceful, and I'm—well—short, round, and fully packed." She patted her hips.

Erin tried not to smile. "What's your point?"

"We're different, that's all. You got the looks, talent, and brains, and I got"— Amy tousled her shoulder-length curly dark hair—"dandruff."

Against her will Erin laughed. "All right, you win. You sure can wear a person down, Amy. I'll go in for you on Saturday. But this is positively, absolutely the last time I bail you out because you've overcommitted."

Amy smiled broadly and gave Erin a quick hug. Then she took a frizzy red clown's wig off her dresser and put it on her head. On her nose she stuck a fat, round red bulb. "What do you think?"

"You look like Bozo."

"Good. I told Miss Hutton I'd do a gig for the Children's Home at Easter."

"I thought you didn't like her."

"She's okay, but don't tell anybody I said so. I like doing crazy things like this and making people laugh. I know it's silly, and it's not half as important as your dancing, but it's me."

"Amy, my dancing is no more important than your acting. You'll be a great actress someday—*if* you ever get serious about life."

Amy gasped in horror. "Oh, I hope I *never* get serious. What would people think?"

"I've got to get back to my homework," Erin said, shaking her head in exasperation.

"Wait a minute." Still wearing the wig and nose, Amy dashed to her desk and picked up a packet of snapshots. "Did I show you these yet? They're the photos Travis and I took on Christmas Day at his house."

Erin tried to keep her expression blank as she sorted through them, but in truth she was tied in knots. Why did she have to be so attracted to him?

Amy leaned over her elbow. "That's the one of him kissing me under the mistletoe. His little brother took it, and I thought Travis was going to kill him."

Erin's heart ached, and she quickly handed the photos back to Amy. "They're nice."

"I don't know why Travis is interested in *me*," Amy mused. "I mean he's only the hottest thing at Berkshire Prep. I think every girl at Briarwood is in love with him."

"Not everyone," Erin said, looking away as she said it.

"Well, of course I didn't mean you. But a lot of them are. Cindy Pitzer for instance." Amy made a face. "She's been telling people she really likes him and that she's going after him."

"I wouldn't worry about it," Erin said. "*You're* the one he's dating."

"True," Amy said with a bright smile. She tossed the photos onto her dresser and turned toward Erin. "Oh, by the way, a couple of Travis's friends have asked me about you. If you ever want to double with us—"

"No," Erin interrupted sharply, too sharply, and Amy gave her a surprised look. "I mean, thanks but no thanks. Between school and dance classes, I haven't got time for dating. You know how much I want to go to Florida State, and the competition's stiff."

"But that's two years away."

"I have to concentrate on one thing at a time."

"Well, if you change your mind . . ."

"You'll be the first to know." Despite Amy's protests Erin returned to her room, but she found she couldn't get back into studying. She thought about Saturday and her promise to work for her sister. Why had she let Amy talk her into it? Why did she always give in to Amy's pleas? "Because she's just *Amy*," Erin explained to the empty room.

With a sense of vengeance, she quickly set her alarm clock for five-thirty, relishing the thought of dragging her sister out of bed for the early rehearsal. At least Amy would be on time for *something*.

On Saturday morning Erin poked through the racks of clothes in her mother's boutique while eyeing the clock. She'd been on duty an hour, and not one customer had stepped through the door. Outside the day looked bleak and blustery, and the parking lot for the small shopping center was nearly deserted. The cool, cloudy day meant there would be few who wanted their cars washed, so the Drama Club's fundraiser would probably be a flop. "Serves Amy right," she muttered.

Erin spied a bright red jumpsuit and impulsively

snatched it off the rack and dashed into a dressing room. She emerged and stood at the three-way mirror. The outfit made her look years older, more sophisticated. "Wow," she mumbled, hardly recognizing herself. She wondered if Travis would think she looked pretty. She closed her eyes and imagined that he was standing next to her.

"Not bad, Erin. You look terrific."

The voice startled Erin. Her eyes flew open wide. In the mirror she saw Travis Sinclair, and he was looking over her shoulder, straight into the glass, straight into her eyes.

Chapter Three

"Travis! I—uh—I didn't hear you come in."

"I know. I'm sorry if I scared you." He glanced around the deserted shop. "Where's Amy? She told me she was working today."

"She took off for the afternoon because of the Drama Club car wash."

Travis snapped his fingers. "Oh yeah, now I remember. She did tell me about it, along with a million other things. You know how Amy is—fastest mouth in the West." He grinned, and Erin's heart beat faster.

"The car wash is at the gas station near Briarwood."

"That's right. I guess I should drive by and get them to wash mine. Not that it needs washing, but if I don't take it, Amy will never get off my case."

Despite what Travis had said, Erin could tell by his tone how fond he was of her sister.

He picked a blouse off a rack and held it up. "Actually, Erin . . . there is something I wanted to ask you."

In spite of herself Erin felt her mouth go dry. "What's that?"

"Amy's birthday. It's two weeks away, and I'm kind of out of ideas for a present. Any suggestions?"

Erin sagged, suddenly aware of how tense she'd become. "What makes you think she gives her wish list to me?"

"I was just thinking that since you're her sister, you could help me pick something special, that's all. I don't care what it costs, just as long as Amy likes it."

"There's nothing you couldn't pick out that she wouldn't like, Travis, but I did see her going through this stuff last week. She found a sweater she was crazy about. Now, let's see . . . which one was it?" Actually, there hadn't been one, but Erin wanted an excuse to be with him.

Travis stood next to Erin, watching her hands push through the rack of clothing. "Hope you can find it," he mumbled.

"Ah, here it is." She held up a bright blue sweater for his inspection, grateful that she was familiar with Amy's tastes.

"Uh—it's real nice." He fingered it. "Soft too."

"It's got angora in it."

"What's that?"

"Rabbit fur."

"You sure she liked it?"

"Positive. But don't tell her I helped you pick it out. It would be better if she thinks you chose it on your own."

Travis nodded. "Fair enough. Can you gift wrap it?"

Erin rang up the sale and showed him an assortment of wrapping paper. "Which do you like best?"

Travis knit his brows and pondered. Erin noticed

how his wavy dark hair complemented his olive complexion and that his eyelashes were long and thick. "This one," he said. She fumbled with the paper, begging her hands to obey her will. He lounged against the counter as she worked.

"Amy talks about you a lot, Erin," Travis said. "All about what a great dancer you are."

"She exaggerates—she just wants to get out of those early-morning rehearsals."

"I guess you know her tricks," he said. "She really does think you're a terrific sister, Erin. You should hire her as a press agent for your dancing career."

"I'm going to college first," she told him, creating a large pink bow from a spool of satin ribbon. "Then I'll go after a professional dancing career. Once I get too old to dance professionally, I can still get a good job teaching dance like Ms. Thornton."

Travis shook his head. "You and Amy sure are different. You have the rest of your life all planned out, and Amy barely makes it from day to day. She just figures that things will work out her way."

"She's not serious enough. You know—single-minded. She can't say no to anybody if they ask her for a favor. So she spreads herself too thin." Suddenly Erin realized that what she was saying might be taken as criticism.

"That's one of the things I like about her," Travis countered. "She's not like other girls. She's never too busy to listen if you want to talk. And nothing's too crazy for her to try."

Erin thought of the clown wig and nose. She

didn't know many girls who'd have the guts to do that kind of spontaneous acting. She knew she wouldn't. Erin sighed, forced a big smile, and held out the neatly wrapped package. "All done."

"Hey, that looks good. Think she'll know I didn't wrap it?"

"I'll never tell," Erin said. When he took the gift, their hands brushed. She drew back quickly as static electricity snapped between them.

"I could say this was a shocking experience," Travis said.

"Don't," Erin said with a groan.

He crossed to the door and turned. "Thanks, Erin, for the help with the gift and the talk. You may be more like Amy than you think."

In an effort to hide her embarrassment, Erin rolled her eyes. "Please don't tell me that. I don't think the world's ready for two Amys." She watched him drive off, and her heart filled with yearning. More than ever she knew she cared about Travis Sinclair. And more than ever she realized that there was nothing she could do about it. Absolutely nothing.

Later at home Erin tried to do her homework, but fireworks from the den kept interrupting her concentration. She couldn't hear much, just the low rumble of her father's voice and an occasional outburst from Amy such as, "Daddy! You can't mean that!" and "That's not fair. I've already made plans," and "It's a stupid old paper!"

She heard doors slamming, Amy's feet running

up the hall, and another door slamming. Whatever ultimatum their father had delivered, Amy certainly hadn't talked him out of it. Erin felt a perverse sense of satisfaction and guilt. She warred with herself. "It's nothing she doesn't deserve. This whole house revolves around Amy. I'll just let her stew about it tonight and ask her about it in the morning."

But guilt won out. Erin sneaked down the hall to Amy's room and tapped on the door. "Can I come in?"

"Sure."

Amy was sniffing and hanging up the phone when Erin entered. The room was in its usual state of disaster. She eased onto the bed. "Bad, huh?"

"The worst." Amy twisted a tissue around her finger. "Daddy's grounded me for the entire weekend. And he says that if I don't finish my history paper by Monday, he won't let me take my driver's test on my birthday next Friday. He'll make me wait a whole month!" Her eyes filled with fresh tears. "Travis and I were supposed to go to a concert tomorrow night, and I just called and told him I couldn't go."

"Oh, Ames," Erin said, using her sister's nickname, "that's a drag."

"It sure is." Amy blew her nose. "Travis really wants to go, and I'm afraid if I don't go with him and Cindy Pitzer finds out, she might try to get him to take her. I couldn't stand the thought of him asking anyone else—especially Cindy." Amy wiped her eyes with her shirtsleeve. "So I came up with an alternate plan."

"Don't ask me to write your paper," Erin warned.

"And I won't cover for you if you try to sneak out your window either."

"I hadn't thought of that. . . ."

"Well don't think about it."

"No, I already talked about it with Travis, and he says it's okay with him if it's okay with you."

"What's okay?"

"I don't want him to go with another girl. And I don't want him to go alone since his buddies all have dates. So I need for him to go with somebody I can trust." Amy turned tear-stained, innocent blue eyes on Erin. "I told him *you'd* go with him."

The whole time Erin was getting ready for the concert, she kept telling herself that she'd done her best to talk Amy out of the idea. Yet deep in her heart, she knew she was glad she was going, and that she was more excited about it than anything she'd done in ages.

"You look super," Amy told her as Erin put the finishing touches on her makeup.

"Thanks."

"I'm jealous," Amy admitted in a small voice.

"Now, just a minute. This whole thing was your idea."

Amy scuffed her foot on the carpet in Erin's bedroom. "I know. But it still matters that you're going instead of me."

Erin kept applying mascara, forcing herself not to catch Amy's eye in the mirror. She was afraid that if she did, Amy would see the truth there. "It's too late to change plans."

"I know." Amy sidled her another look. "I didn't expect you to look so pretty either."

Erin stopped the mascara wand in midair and turned from her vanity table. "Why, Amy? I've worn this outfit a hundred times before."

"Maybe so, but somehow tonight you look different . . . better . . . sort of *glowing.*"

Erin felt her cheeks redden. "Don't be silly. I'm excited about the concert, that's all. How's the paper coming?"

Amy grimaced. "Fine, if you like researching the Crimean War. Too bad it's not out on video. I could watch it on the VCR and then write about it."

"Oh, Ames, you're impossible. Maybe when you're set to storm Broadway, someone will have written a play about it that you can star in. Then won't you be glad you read all about it?"

They both laughed. In the distance the doorbell sounded. "That's Travis," Amy said, jumping to her feet and rushing to the door. "Let me prepare him for the shock of someone actually ready to go out on time."

"Take your time. I won't hurry."

"Thanks, Erin. I really do mean it. I want you both to have a ball."

Alone, Erin began to feel guilty. "It's what Amy wants," she told her mirror image. "Travis likes Amy, and he's just taking me because he wants to see the concert." She was positive of those two things. But she made certain that her wheat-colored hair was perfectly combed and that she used an extra spritz of her best perfume before she left the room.

The concert music was too loud and the civic center smoky, and by the time Erin and Travis got back to the Bennett's house, Erin had a splitting headache. They had barely gotten in the door when Amy started firing questions at them. "How was it? Was it loud—I mean *really* loud? And who else did you see there? Don't spare any details."

Travis gave her a hug and a smile, the first genuine smile Erin had seen on his face that evening. "Awesome," he told Amy.

Erin felt slighted. He hadn't acted as if he'd had an awesome time. Amy pulled him into the living room, where a bowl of fresh popcorn and cans of soda waited on the coffee table. "Sit down and start talking."

Erin followed hesitantly, suddenly feeling like an extra with no lines to read. A lump formed in her throat, and she tried to wash it down. She heard Amy and Travis talking, saw their heads close together and their hands touching. Without a word she turned and went to her room.

Chapter Four

"You've got to get them all out in one breath, or your wish won't come true," Mrs. Bennett reminded Amy as she set the birthday cake on the dining-room table.

"No problem there," Travis said. "We all know that she's full of hot air."

Erin laughed along with her mother and father as Amy punched his arm. "There're *only* sixteen candles," she said. "This'll be a cinch."

Mr. Bennett flipped off the light switch, and the fire from the candles reflected off Amy's face. Erin saw how radiant her sister looked. She felt ashamed of how she'd acted on the night of the concert, keeping to herself once Travis had gone home and not wanting to talk much about the night.

"What flavor's the cake?" Travis asked.

"Devil's food with white boiled icing," Mrs. Bennett said. "It's Amy's favorite."

"Devil's food? I should have guessed." Everyone laughed again.

Amy filled her lungs and puffed out her cheeks. Mr. Bennett snapped a photo just as she blew on the candles, and in seconds all that remained were spirals of smoke. Amy stood and took a bow. "And you doubted I could get them all in one puff." She held out her hands. "Okay. No one eats until I get my presents."

"Not fair," Mr. Bennett called.

"Life isn't fair," Amy said with a grin.

"Well, I want my cake, so I'm not holding out," Travis said, and forked over the box Erin had so carefully wrapped weeks before.

Erin watched as Amy tore into the paper. So much like Amy, she thought. Erin would have carefully removed the tape from each end and neatly folded the paper back. Amy held up the blue sweater and squealed. "It's gorgeous! I've never seen anything so pretty. Thanks a million."

Travis offered Erin a questioning glance, but she only shrugged her shoulders as if to say, "Isn't that just like Amy to act as if it's the first time she's laid eyes on it?"

Her parents gave Amy a generous gift certificate for clothes and a professional makeup kit. "To hold all that clown stuff," Mrs. Bennett explained.

"It's fabulous," Amy said. "Now I'll look like a real pro!" She hugged them both, then turned toward Erin. "Well?" she asked.

"Well what?"

"Well where's my present from you?"

"*Moi?*" Erin asked flapping her eyelashes. "Didn't I get you a gift for your last birthday?"

Amy danced up and down. "Give me my present, or I won't show up for the recital next Saturday night."

Erin rolled her eyes and leaned toward Travis. "A trained seal could read the part."

"Could not!" Amy protested.

"And be on time for the rehearsals."

Amy made a face. "I'll never be late again. Promise."

"Never?"

Amy crossed her heart, then leaned into Travis's other side. "It's my party, and I'll lie if I want to." They all groaned over her pun.

Erin handed over a shoe-sized box, which Amy shook. "It rattles," she said, shredding the paper. She lifted out a shiny key chain. A key and a small rectangular box dangled from one end, and a large solid-brass letter *A* from the other.

"Let me explain," Erin said, taking the chain from Amy's hand. "First, the key is to my car, which I will let you borrow."

"You mean you're going to let me use *your* car? Thanks, Erin. Thanks a lot."

"On very rare occasions," Erin emphasized.

Amy turned to her father. "Does this mean I won't be getting my Porsche this year?"

"The dealer was back-ordered, so we thought we'd hold off for a while," he told her with a straight face.

She swung around to face Erin, who continued. "This," she pointed to the small box on the chain, "is something that you need in order to keep track of the keys." Erin crossed to the far side of the room and put the keys on the edge of the buffet. "Now whistle," she told Amy.

Her sister obliged, and the box let out a high-pitched whine. "If you ever misplace your keys, Amy—of course we all realize that will never happen." The others joined in with shouts of, "Never!" and "Not Amy."

"If you can't find them, all you have to do is whistle," Erin interrupted.

Amy clapped gleefully. "I love it! Oh Erin, it's super." She bolted out of the dining room, and in a minute they heard her whistle and the box whine.

Mrs. Bennett offered Erin an approving nod. "Looks like you've found the perfect gift. And it's nice of you to share your car."

Erin couldn't help but feel pleased with her choice. Travis caught her eye, and the approval she saw there caused her pulse to quicken. Mr. Bennett yelled out, "Amy, where are you? Are you going to cut this cake, or are we supposed to take chunks out of it with our bare hands?"

"I'll do it," she said. "But I get the part with the most icing."

Mr. Bennett handed the camera to Travis. "Can you get a shot of us together? I intend to have plenty of pictures to embarrass Amy with when she's a refined old lady."

Travis looked through the viewfinder and aimed. "Squeeze in tighter." The Bennetts bunched around Amy, who hunched low and peeked from behind the cake with a silly grin. "You've got frosting on your nose, Amy," he said. "I'll wait while you wipe it off."

Erin muttered, "All we ever do around here is wait on Amy."

Amy crossed her eyes, and Travis snapped the shutter.

On Friday after school Erin found Shara in one of the music rooms, practicing her songs for the upcoming recital. Shara's haunting, lyrical voice sent goose bumps up Erin's arms. "I thought I'd better get some extra practice time in," Shara said, signaling Erin into the tiny, soundproof room.

Erin wished Amy would take her part in the recital half as seriously. "No hurry," Erin told her. "I'll wait." She sat in a metal chair.

"I'm glad you're sleeping over tonight. With my mom visiting her sister and Dad working late at the hospital, I dreaded the thought of being home alone." Shara said. "After dinner we can go to a movie at the mall and then maybe do some cruising."

"Cruising at the mall? Only nerds hang around the mall on Friday night."

"Now don't be negative. You never know."

"*I* know," Erin said.

"Just remember, Erin, Spring Fling comes up after Easter, and I for one intend to go this year. That requires meeting somebody to ask."

To Shara it was all so simple, but Erin found it far more complicated. She didn't want to attend the big Briarwood extravaganza with just anybody. She wanted to go with a guy who mattered to her. Unfortunately, the only guy who mattered was off-limits. "What about you and Kenny? You were seeing a lot of him before Christmas."

"Kenny's old news. He was nice enough, but sort of dull, if you know what I mean."

"And you don't want to go with a bunch of girls like we did last year? I'm hurt."

Shara made a face. "No thanks. I want to buy something ridiculously expensive and watch some guy's eyeballs pop out when I walk through the door."

"If that's all you want, wear your birthday suit."

"If all I wear is my birthday suit, he'll run off screaming," Shara grumbled. "Don't you want to go? You're a dancer, after all."

"There's no similarity between that kind of dancing and the modern and jazz that I like to do."

"But picture yourself slow-dancing with someone tall, dark, and sexy." Shara did a few spins around the cramped room. "Then later, in the moonlight . . ."

It was all too easy for Erin to picture. "Sorry, Shara. I can't imagine meeting Mr. Right at the mall."

"You have no imagination." Erin smiled. The problem was, she had too much imagination. "I'll bet Amy is taking Travis," Shara said.

"She's already on me to help her pick out something at the boutique. Her taste in formal wear is as crazy as she is, and so far she can't settle on anything."

"Knowing Amy, she'll turn up in her clown makeup," Shara said.

"Knowing Amy, she'll be so late that everyone will have gone home by the time she gets there."

Shara chuckled and picked up her books. "Come on, let's go. If we hurry, we can grab a bite at my house, then go to the early show. That'll leave us about an hour to hang around before the mall closes."

Hadn't Shara heard a word Erin had said? But rather than argue, Erin grabbed her things and left with her friend. "Don't forget, we have rehearsal tomorrow morning," she told Shara.

The blond-haired girl groaned. "You're a regular slave driver, Erin."

"The recital's next Saturday night, and we're going to be best in the show."

"Is Amy supposed to meet us at the studio? She'll be late."

"Not tomorrow," Erin said with a smug grin. "I set her alarm ahead an hour. I figure that should put her there right on time."

"You sneaky devil," Shara said with a laugh.

Erin tapped her forehead with her finger. "There's more than one way to outwit my sister's internal clock. You just have to use your brain and be creative. Like it or not, time is where people exist between living and dying. Even Amy Sue Bennett has to punch a time clock, just like the rest of us mere mortals."

"That's deep," Shara said with mock seriousness.

"That's reality," Erin countered, giving her friend a playful shove. "So get a move on it before time runs out on us and the mall closes."

Chapter Five

It rained the night of the recital, and Erin was afraid attendance would be down, so she kept peeking from behind the massive red curtain to watch the audience file down the aisles. By the time the program started, there were no empty seats in the theater.

Her number was last on the program, and as the curtain lifted for her performance, she sensed hundreds of eyes on her, making her adrenaline pump. Earlier she'd felt as if she were tied in knots, but now, in the hushed atmosphere of the darkened theater, she was charged—completely calm, yet full of power for the dance.

Amy, dressed all in black, stood behind a Lucite podium at the far left corner of the stage. The elegant leather book lay open to her place. The music started and Shara sang. Erin arched her back, poised on pointe upstage, then walked on a diagonal to center stage. With perfect timing Shara's song crescendoed, and Amy read from Psalm 139.

"Oh Lord, thou has searched me and known me. . . ." Erin began a controlled series of *balances*. "I will praise thee, for I am fearfully and wonderfully made. . . . My substance was not hid from thee, when I was made in secret." As Amy read excerpts, Erin spun faster—her back erect, her arms forming a circle in front of her. The words became her music now. She leapt, executing a perfect spin in the air, landed, and dipped backward until her long hair brushed the floor as Amy read: "And lead me in the way everlasting." She lost all sense of time until the last strains of the music faded and she posed dramatically in the center of the stage, with only the spotlight surrounding her.

Applause erupted, pulling her back to reality. She rose and blinked as the houselights came up, and smiling, she grasped Amy's and Shara's hands and bowed. Once the curtain closed, the three girls collapsed into hugs and squeals of relief. After weeks of work it was over. Erin could scarcely believe it. The other performers converged from the wings offering congratulations.

Ms. Thornton swept through the ranks saying, "Wonderful performance, ladies, really outstanding. Every one of you was spectacular. Now if your parents start coming backstage, don't let them hang around too long. After all, we have a party to throw."

They scurried toward the dressing rooms, where Erin plopped on a metal chair in front of the vanity mirror and reached for her cold cream. The girl next to her, a sophomore, said, "You were sensational, Erin."

There was no mistaking the admiration on the girl's face. "Thanks," Erin told her.

"Aren't we a super team?" Amy asked as she

dragged a chair over and positioned it between Erin and the other girl. "Pass your cold cream, please."

Slightly annoyed, Erin asked, "I thought you brought your own. Where's that fancy kit Mom and Dad bought you for your birthday?"

Amy shrugged and smeared the cream on her face. "I guess I was in such a hurry to be on time, I left it on my bed."

Erin rolled her eyes. "Oh, Amy . . ."

"But I remembered my regular makeup." She grinned and slathered on more of the greasy cream. "How long's this party supposed to last?"

"All evening. Why?"

"'Cause I told Travis to pick me up at eleven."

"You're going out? It's raining like crazy outside. Does Mom know?"

"Mom gave me permission."

"Oh," Erin said, annoyed. Amy was just barely sixteen, and already their mother was changing the curfew rules for her.

"We're going to the latest Freddy Krueger flick. It doesn't start until midnight." Amy looked absolutely comical sitting talking with her sister while her stage makeup ran in streaks down her face.

One of the girls pointed at Amy and started laughing. "Take a look in the mirror, Amy," she said. Another dancer said to Erin, "Amy's such a riot. It must be a blast living with her."

"It's just nonstop laughs around our house," Erin said, smiling stiffly. She faced the mirror and studied her exotic makeup. The eye shadow made her look older, more glamorous. *No matter what I do or say, the spotlight always turns to Amy,* she thought. *Maybe if I leave on this makeup, I'll become somebody more exciting than Erin Bennett.*

Amy reached in front of Erin for a box of tissues. "Listen, if Ms. Thornton misses me, will you cover for me?"

Erin suddenly remembered the award Ms. Thornton had planned to give Amy. It would serve her right if she left before she got it. She started to hint that it might be best if Amy didn't run off with Travis before the party was over but then peevishly decided against it. "Sure, Amy. I'll cover."

"Thanks. You're a true sister." Amy removed the last of the cold cream and stared hard at the mirror. "Good grief, where'd my face disappear to?" She made a production of looking under the long vanity table, beneath jars, and through some of the tabletop clutter while the other girls laughed and kidded her. Finally she retrieved her purse and pulled out a makeup pouch. "Here it is! I found it!"

"Stop being such a show-off," Erin said crossly.

"Gosh, Erin, I'm sorry. Am I embarrassing you?" Amy asked sincerely.

Erin felt her face flush. Some of the other girls had heard, and she knew she must have come across as a prima donna. "Of course not."

"I'd never do that on purpose, you know."

The dressing-room door opened, and Ms. Thornton peered inside. "Let's get a move on ladies. Everything's set up on stage, and it's already ten o'clock."

The room burst into activity, and soon Erin found herself alone. She still hadn't even begun to remove her stage makeup and dress for the party. She sighed and stood, glanced around at the jumble of duffel bags and clothes, and wondered where hers was buried. She hated being late. Her irritation with Amy returned. It had been the news about her sister's date with Travis that had started it all.

In the mirror she eyed her costume. The gold bangle earrings and the beautiful scarf tied around her hips made her remember the day she'd been alone with him in the boutique and he'd told her she looked pretty. Now the scarf looked limp and sad, and the jewelry seemed tarnished. Why couldn't she be the one with the date? She was older than Amy. Why couldn't Travis Sinclair be interested in her?

"Stop it," she demanded of her reflection. "Just stop wishing for the impossible." Erin found her duffel bag, quickly removed the elaborate makeup with cold cream, reapplied her everyday makeup, and changed into jeans and a sweater.

The stage was bathed in fuchsia and gold lights, and a sheet cake sat on a table decorated with balloons and banners. Ms. Thornton had thought of everything. Shara wove through a group of girls and came up to Erin, handing her a piece of cake on a napkin. "What kept you? I changed in the other dressing room."

"Amy got to chattering, and before you knew it, everybody was ready but me."

Shara toasted Erin with her cake. "We were a hit, weren't we?"

Erin gave a lackluster shrug. "I guess so."

"What's bugging you?"

"Nothing."

Shara arched an eyebrow. "Amy?" She asked, intuitively.

"She's such a pain sometimes."

"So what's Amy done this time? She did a terrific job on the readings for your dance."

"I know," Erin shrugged, frustrated because she could never put into words how she really felt about Amy. Unable to think of anything, she took a bite out of her cake.

"Having a good time?" Ms. Thornton asked as she walked over to where they stood.

"Super," Erin and Shara said in unison.

"I really think your number was outstanding, Erin," Ms. Thornton said. Shara excused herself, and Ms. Thornton continued. "You just keep growing and maturing as a dancer."

"Thank you," was all Erin could manage. Her instructor's opinion meant more to her than anybody's.

Ms. Thornton studied Erin thoughtfully, then said, "In fact, I'd like to recommend you to the Wolftrap Dance Academy in Washington. The director is always looking for the brightest and the best. I'm sure I could get you in on scholarship this summer. Of course, Allen will want you to turn professional and go to New York." A knowing smile crossed Ms. Thornton's face. "But I know you're geared for college, and after you get your degree, you can still pursue a professional career if you want."

A dance scholarship with Wolftrap! Erin didn't know what to say. Ms. Thornton put her hand on Erin's shoulder. "We'll discuss it in more detail later, but I'd like you to start thinking about it now."

Before Erin could utter a word, one of the girls came over. "Ms. Thornton, we're out of sodas."

"Already? I thought I bought plenty."

The girl shrugged. "I guess we were really thirsty."

Ms. Thornton puckered her brow and spoke almost to herself. "Well, I'll just have to run to the store."

"I'll go," Erin offered.

"I don't know. . . ."

"I don't mind. My car's right outside."

Ms. Thornton glanced around at the stage full of girls before turning again to Erin. "If you're sure you don't mind. Here, let me give you some money."

Erin tagged after the teacher, who retrieved her purse and handed her some cash. "Buy a whole case. That should hold us for the rest of the party."

"I'll be back in a flash." The news about the scholarship had lifted her spirits so much that Erin felt she could have flown to the store.

"Don't forget your raincoat," Ms. Thornton called before Erin could open the backstage door.

"Oh yeah." She dashed to the dressing room,

found her coat, and was again almost out the door when Amy stopped her.

"Where are you going?"

"To the store. We're out of sodas."

Amy grabbed Erin's arm. "Oh let me go! Please. I've had my license for a whole week, and I still haven't had a chance to use the car."

Erin paused. "But I told Ms. Thornton I'd go."

"She won't mind if I go instead. You said I could drive your car as part of my birthday present."

"How about if we go together?"

"Ugh!" Amy made a face. "I want to drive by myself this time. Pretty please? I'll be your best friend."

Erin thought about the cold, damp March weather and about her car heater that was on the fritz. And about how much she'd love to corner Shara and tell her about the Wolftrap Academy and the dance scholarship. "If I let you go for me, don't mess around. Get the sodas and come right back. Okay?"

"Don't worry. I'm meeting Travis, remember?" Erin remembered. "I'll be back in a jiffy."

Amy started out the door, and a blast of damp wind hit them both, making Erin shiver. "Where's your coat?"

"I think I left it in the dressing room."

"You'll get soaked. Here take mine. And here's money for the sodas. Get a whole case!" She yelled as Amy jumped over puddles and dodged raindrops.

She watched as Amy struggled with the car's stubborn door before climbing inside and starting the engine. In the glow of the mercury lamppost, the car looked hard and colorless. Amy waved and turned toward the street, the headlights' sweeping arc cutting through the darkness and the pouring rain. Not knowing why, Erin stood at the door and watched until the taillights had disappeared completely into the night.

Chapter Six

"What're you doing here by the door?" Shara's question interrupted Erin's vigilance over the parking lot.

"Just watching Amy. She went to the store to get more sodas." Erin stepped inside, and the heavy door snapped shut.

"You look like it's bothering you."

"Ms. Thornton asked me to go, and I let Amy badger me into going instead."

"So?"

Erin shrugged. "Nothing, I guess." She looked at Shara and suddenly remembered what Ms. Thornton had said about the Wolftrap Academy. "Hey, guess what? Ms. Thornton really liked my dance, and she's going to recommend me to the director at Wolftrap."

Shara's eyes grew wider as Erin told her. "That's excellent. Would your parents let you go to Washington for the summer?"

"They'd better! I figure if I work really hard between now and June, I can convince them that this is really important to me. I mean, this is the chance of a lifetime. Wolftrap was started by people who were trained by Martha Graham." Erin said the name of the modern-dance pioneer reverently. "Can you imagine? *Me* working with teachers like *that*."

Shara seemed sufficiently impressed. "I guess it'd be like me getting a recording contract. You're lucky you have someone like Ms. Thornton helping you."

Erin knew that was true, and she was determined to fulfill Ms. Thornton's faith in her.

"Hey Erin! Shara!" Donna Gaines called. "Come on out here. Ms. Thornton's gonna show us the tape of the show."

The girls hurried back to the main stage, where everyone was sitting on the floor, eyes glued to a TV that had been propped on the table beside the half-eaten cake. Ms. Thornton asked, "Back with the sodas, Erin?"

"I—um—I let Amy go get them for us."

The rest of the dance troupe moaned. Someone said, "Amy! Good grief, the party'll be over before we see her again."

"Yeah," someone else added. "Amy has two speeds—slow and no-show."

Laughter rippled through the group. Erin felt as if she should say something in her sister's defense, but nothing came to mind. After all, it was true.

"Settle down, ladies," Ms. Thornton directed. "She'll be here eventually. Let's start the tape."

Erin dropped to the floor next to Shara and drew her knees against her chest, watching the screen intently. The sound quality was tinny, but the images were clear and sharp. One after the other the dance numbers proceeded across the screen. The girls pointed at themselves, with several groaning over mistakes. By the time her number started, Erin's palms were sweating. She wanted so much for it to be good.

On the tape she heard Amy's voice and vaguely wondered why it was taking her sister so long to return. Erin concentrated on her movements, evaluating them critically. Her leaps were high, but she decided she needed more arch to her back. She made a mental note to work on flexibility. Could she ever be ready for a place like Wolftrap?

Applause sounded as the tape ran out and electronic snow splattered over the screen. Everyone began to stand and stretch, and Erin pulled herself up too.

"Is that someone pounding on the backstage door?" Ms. Thornton asked.

"Maybe it's Amy," somebody suggested. "Her timing's perfect. The party's over."

"I'll get it," Erin called, rushing for the door, determined to throttle her sister for blowing such a simple mission. She jerked open the door and looked right into Travis Sinclair's face.

"Where's Amy?" he asked. Erin realized that Travis was mad. "She said she'd be waiting right here by the door. I knocked real quiet, but she didn't open it, so I had to beat on it."

"Gosh, Travis, is it eleven o'clock already?"

"Eleven-fifteen. Hey, Erin, it's wet and cold out here. Do you think I could come in?"

Flustered, Erin held open the door, and a dripping Travis stepped inside. "This was supposed to be a subtle exit," he grumbled. "Now it looks like half the world's in on it."

Erin turned to see the Terpsicord girls as well as Ms. Thornton emerging from the backstage shadows. Ms. Thornton asked, "What's going on?"

Erin felt her cheeks grow hot. How did Amy always manage to put her on the spot? "Um—this is Travis Sinclair. He was supposed to pick Amy up and take her—er—home," she finished lamely, hating herself for lying.

Ms. Thornton looked doubtful. "I was about to give out some awards for our work here tonight," she said.

Travis shifted, jamming his hands into the pockets of his trench coat. "I could wait here by the door."

Ms. Thornton glanced at her watch. "It's late, Erin. What time did Amy leave anyway?"

"Ten-thirty."

"Even Amy should have been back by now."

A small shiver of fear shot up Erin's spine. "I can't imagine what's keeping her. Maybe she had car trouble. I mean, my car's old, and sometimes it gets cranky."

"We could drive around and look for her," Travis suggested.

Several girls offered to take their cars and look also. "No," Ms. Thornton said. "You all stay put. Erin, you and Travis go. But be back here in thirty minutes whether you find her or not."

Erin agreed and ran behind Travis through a pelting rain to where his car was parked. Her teeth were chattering, and Travis, fiddling with the heater buttons, asked, "Which way did she head?"

Erin pointed, and he drove out of the lot and down a dark, deserted road. Erin chewed her bottom lip, peering through the side window. It was hard to see through the film of rain, so she kept rubbing the palm of her hand over the glass, even though it didn't help. "I should have never let her go in my place," she said miserably.

"Don't worry. Knowing Amy, she ran out of gas and is sitting in some diner munching out."

Erin was touched by his attempt to comfort her, but she knew that she'd had a full tank of gas. The rhythmic slap of the wipers matched Erin's heartbeat. *Steady,* she told herself. *Everything's fine*. "I don't see any cars broken down along the road," Travis said after he'd driven several miles. "What store do you think she might have gone to for the drinks?"

"I don't know. There's a bunch of minimarts on this street and two grocery stores farther north."

"Then we'll stop at all of them and ask if anyone's seen her." Travis made a U-turn and headed back toward Briarwood. "We'll start at the one closest to the school and work our way down." Erin clutched her coat—Amy's coat—closer to her body. "Are you cold?" Travis asked, turning up the heater.

She was shivering, but she was sweating too. "Thanks," she mumbled.

They stopped at each brightly lit store and described Amy, and each time the sales help shook their heads. In one of the larger grocery stores, Travis talked to the store manager while Erin canvased each checkout girl. The answer was always the same: "Sorry, haven't seen her."

After having no better luck at the second of the big supermarkets, Travis sat in the car brooding and staring out at the falling rain. "We'd better keep going," Erin told him.

He turned to face her in the bucket seat. "We're ten miles from the school, Erin. She wouldn't have come this far."

Erin grew agitated. "You don't know that for sure. It's too soon to give up."

"I'm not giving up. It's just that she must have gone somewhere else."

"But where?" By now Erin was really scared, because even Amy wasn't this irresponsible. They sat in silence. The rain beat on the metal roof, and Erin felt a headache coming on.

"Maybe she went home," Travis ventured.

Instantly Erin brightened. "I'll bet you're right. She probably wanted to change clothes before going to the movie. Let's go check my house."

Travis started the engine, and Erin caught sight of the digital clock on the dashboard. "Ms. Thornton!" she cried. "We promised her we'd be back in half an hour."

"Is there a phone at the theater?"

"Yes."

"Then we'll go back and call your house from there."

"The more I think about it, I'll bet that's just what happened," Erin insisted. "Honestly, my sister can be *so* thoughtless sometimes. I know you like her 'free spirit,' Travis, but you've got to admit that sometimes she's her own worst enemy."

They returned to the back parking lot of the theater, and Erin jumped out before Travis had turned off the engine. She raced through the rain, stepping into puddles and feeling the water sop through her sneakers and thick socks. She forgot to turn up her coat collar, and cold water ran down her neck. She pounded on the stage door, and it opened immediately.

"Did you find her?" Ms. Thornton asked.

Travis came through the door, and it banged hard behind him. "No luck," he said. "We hit every store for miles, but no one remembered seeing her."

"We thought that she might have gone home for some reason," Erin said, her voice sounding breathy. "I thought I'd call my house from here."

"Of course." Ms. Thornton led the way to a small office and flipped on the light.

The glare stung Erin's eyes, and the room seemed to take on a surrealistic glow. She picked up the telephone receiver and punched her number. "Where'd everybody go?" she asked, counting the rings.

"I sent the girls home, but I promised to start the phone chain once we heard something." The phone chain was Ms. Thornton's method of dispensing information to the dance troupe. She called one person, who called another, and so on down the line until everyone got the message.

By the tenth ring Erin realized no one was going to answer. A hard, heavy sensation lodged in her stomach. "No one's home," she said.

"Had your parents planned to go out?"

"No." Erin's voice had become a whisper. She hung up the phone. "Something's wrong, Ms. Thornton."

Ms. Thornton put her arm around Erin's shoulder. "Let's not jump to any conclusions. There're lots of possible explanations—" She was interrupted by the sound of someone banging on the back door.

The three of them ran toward it, but Travis got there first and yanked on the handle. A blast of wind and rain blew in with a short, plump woman.

Erin blinked. "Inez!" she cried, recognizing her mother's sales assistant from the boutique. "What are you doing here?"

Inez wrung her hands and grabbed Erin by the forearms. She was crying. "Erin, there's been an accident."

"Mom and Dad?" Erin almost gagged.

"They're at County's emergency room. It's Amy, Erin. Amy's been in a terrible wreck."

Chapter Seven

Erin would remember the ride to the hospita
with Travis as a series of dreamlike impressions—rair
falling, the red gold aura of mercury vapor lamp
flashing past the windows, the stuffy heat in the car
the silence between her and Travis, the thudding o
her heart. None of it seemed real. Yet when Travi
turned the car into the entrance marked Emergenc
Only, Erin recoiled. The building loomed tall and for-
bidding, not at all friendly. Somewhere inside Am
lay, hurt and maybe in pain, and that frightened Erir
even more.

The emergency waiting room was a zoo, with to
many people crammed into too small an area. Babie
cried, and people who looked very sick slumped ir
wheelchairs. Erin searched for her parents. "Wher
are they?" she asked.

"Maybe we should ask someone," Travis suggested.

"I'd rather look for them myself," she told him
darting up a hallway like a mouse caught in a maze
The smell of alcohol and disinfectant was making he
nauseous. Nurses passed her, too busy to stop, so Erir
ventured up another corridor, where she saw he
mother and father huddled outside a closed door.

She ran toward them. Her father's face was the color of chalk, and her mother's mascara made dark smudged rings beneath her eyes. Erin threw herself into her mother's arms. "What happened? How's Amy?"

"No one's sure what happened," Mrs. Bennett's voice sounded tight and very controlled. "The police said that she lost control of the car, it hit a tree, and her head hit the steering wheel. Evidently she didn't have her seat belt on."

"Amy hates the shoulder strap," Erin mumbled. "Have the doctors told you anything? How long has she been in there?"

"Maybe an hour. The ER doctor came out once and said that since it's a head injury, they've called in a neurologist. We're waiting for him to tell us something now."

"But she's all right, isn't she? I mean they're probably just stitching up cuts or something, right?"

"All they told us is that it's a head injury," Mrs. Bennett said again. She let go of Erin and stared at her full in the face. "What was she doing driving in the rain at night anyway?"

Erin's voice began to quaver, and she clenched her fists to control her shaking. "She went out for sodas for the party. We ran out."

"What's the matter with Ms. Thornton? Why would she send Amy? She's only had her license for a week. I always considered Thornton to be a responsible person."

Erin squeezed her mother's arm to stop her angry

tirade. "I–it wasn't her fault. I was supposed to go, but Amy begged me to let her go instead." Erin dropped her gaze to the floor, where shiny tiles marched in neat, clean green-and-white formations. The pattern began to blur as tears filled her eyes. "I–I let her take my car."

Mrs. Bennett grabbed Erin's shoulders and shook her. "Erin! How could you have been so thoughtless? You know Amy's not an experienced driver."

"I know. . . . I'm sorry. . . ."

"I've always counted on you, Erin, to have common sense. I would expect Amy to be careless, but *you*!"

Her mother's face was livid, and Erin shrank back toward the wall as her father stepped over and put his arm around her. "Stop it, Marian. It's not Erin's fault. It was an accident."

Erin huddled against her father's side, watching her mother's eyes blaze and her lips compress into a line. Mrs. Bennett turned and walked away down the corridor. "D–daddy . . ." Erin buried her face in her father's coat. It smelled of rain and pipe tobacco.

"It's all right, Princess," he said soothingly. "She's upset. She doesn't really blame you." He stroked Erin's hair absently. "We were getting ready to watch the eleven o'clock news when the cop came and told us. He gave us a police escort down here."

"Inez came to the theater to tell me."

"We figured it would be better than having the police come tell you. And even if I could have reached you by phone, I didn't want you to hear it that way."

He glanced both ways down the hall. "Where is Inez anyway?"

"I guess she's out front with Travis. I rode here with him. Maybe I should tell them something."

"Go on. I'll talk to your mother."

The waiting room was even more crowded now. It was warm too, heavy with the distinct odor of pain and sickness.

"Erin, what's happening?" Travis asked. She felt her knees buckle, and he guided her to a chair that was miraculously vacant.

"We don't know much yet. Amy lost control of the car, and it hit a tree. A specialist is in with her because it's a head injury."

Travis knelt beside her, and Inez hovered at her elbow. Erin twisted her hands in her lap. They felt like blocks of ice. "She's hurt real bad, Travis. I can feel it."

"Maybe not. Maybe she just needs stitches, or some bones are broken. It takes time for them to check her over and figure it all out. I came here with a broken arm once, and it took forever for them to check me over and send me to X-ray and everything."

"This hospital has a good reputation," Inez interjected in a soft Spanish-accented voice. "The trauma unit was featured in the newspaper last month. You know, they have a heliport on the roof, and they fly in patients from all over Florida because the best doctors work right here."

"I hope she isn't hurting," Erin whispered.

"Don't worry, they give you a shot for pain," Travis said.

"Amy hates shots. When we were little, I always had to go first, and if I cried, nothing could make Amy take her shot. One time it took two nurses and Mom to help hold her down. After that I didn't cry again." The memory was so vivid that Erin could suddenly smell the isopropyl alcohol and hear Amy shrieking. "Maybe I should go back to Mom and Dad."

"You'll let us know when you hear from the doctor, won't you?" Travis asked.

"Yes." Erin saw fear in the darkness of his eyes. "As soon as I know anything." She hurried out of the waiting area and returned to her parents.

"I didn't mean to blame you, Erin," Mrs. Bennett said the minute Erin appeared.

"I know, Mom." But truthfully Erin felt guilty. She never should have let Amy talk her out of going to the store, or she should have at least gone with her.

Mrs. Bennett leaned against the wall. Mr. Bennett asked his wife, "Would you like some coffee?"

"No, I'd like a cigarette."

Erin knew that her mother had stopped smoking three years ago. "There's a soda machine in the other corridor," she said, trying to take her mother's mind off the nerveracking wait. "I could get you something cold."

"No. Thanks," she added as an afterthought. "What's taking so long?"

Erin was wondering the same thing. Her stomach felt queasy, and her head was throbbing. Down the hall doors swung open, and a tall man in a white medical coat emerged. Erin tensed. She knew he was coming for them.

"I'm Dr. DuPree, your daughter's neurologist," the man said when he approached. Introductions were made, but then the doctor's attitude turned crisp and professional. "Your daughter has suffered a massive head trauma."

"Amy," Erin blurted, not sure why she wanted him to know. "My sister's name is Amy."

Through black-rimmed glasses his blue eyes studied her kindly. "Amy is stable now. We've got her on a ventilator—that's a machine that breathes for her."

Erin's heart squeezed as if fingers had grabbed it. "Why?"

"We've done a CAT scan. That's a special X-ray of her brain," he explained. "Right now there's a great deal of swelling, and we can't determine the extent of her head injury. But she can't breathe on her own."

Erin's mother gave a little gasp, and Dr. DuPree turned his attention to Erin's parents. "I believe in being completely honest with my patients and their families. I won't lie to you, but I won't give you false hope either. Amy's condition is very serious. I'm having her moved up to Neuro-ICU, where she'll be monitored around the clock. We'll run another CAT scan in a couple of days."

He used such phrases as "severe contusion" and "intracranial pressure" and "diuretics to reduce fluid," but the words slid around in Erin's mind. The only thing that made any sense was when Dr. DuPree said, "She's stable, but comatose."

For a moment no one spoke; then both her parents began to talk at once, questions upon questions, which Dr. DuPree answered. Erin backed away, picturing Amy in a hospital bed surrounded by strangers. "I want to see my sister," she demanded, interrupting the dialogue between Dr. DuPree and her parents. "I want to stay with Amy."

Dr. DuPree took one of her hands. His palm was warm, and she noticed that his fingers were long and immaculate. "There's a waiting room next to Neuro-ICU for families of critical patients. All of you can stay there tonight."

Erin's dad said he'd talk to Inez and Travis, then meet them upstairs. Her mother kept firing questions at the doctor during the ride up the elevator to the seventh floor. Erin steeled her body and emotions with her dancer's iron discipline.

Hospitals and doctors help people, she told herself as she approached the solid door of the Neuro-ICU area. *Amy will be out of here in no time.* She stared at the door, while behind her Dr. DuPree and her mother waited for her to push it open.

"People come out of comas don't they, Dr. DuPree?" she asked. Erin shoved open the door, not waiting for his reply, because deep down she was too terrified to hear his answer.

Chapter Eight

Neuro-ICU was a large room with seven beds and a central desk where nurses kept close watch over patients who had head and brain injuries. It was a netherworld of shadows illuminated by green and amber blips, of machines linked with lines and tubes, and of hissing sounds and electronic beeps keeping perfect cadence. Erin met the night nurse, Laurie, who took her and Mrs. Bennett to a more private room, separated only by a glass partition from the larger area.

"We have three other patients up here now," Laurie said, but Erin only half heard her because she couldn't take her eyes off her sister. Amy's head was swathed in gauze, and a tube protruded from her mouth. Too overwhelmed to speak, Erin stood by the bed and blinked back tears. Her hand reached out, then drew back.

"Don't be afraid; you can touch her," Laurie said.

"She doesn't even look hurt. She just looks like she's asleep."

"The only damage is to her brain. By tommorow you'll be able to see swelling in her face. Her eye area will probably turn black-and-blue."

Erin gently stroked Amy's cheek, careful not to brush against the apparatus. She hoped to see her sister's eyelids flutter, knowing that Amy hated being tickled. "What are all these tubes and wires for?"

"The oral tube is her ventilator. That wire is taped to her chest and leads to her heart monitor, and that tube in the back of her hand is an IV. She has a catheter too."

"My poor little girl," Mrs. Bennett whispered from the other side of Amy's bed. Erin swallowed hard and tried not to look at her mother. If she did, she knew she'd lose it.

"You can stay with her for now," Laurie said softly. "The waiting room is right down the hall. You can come in and out of here to check on your daughter whenever you want."

"I'll wait here for my husband," Mrs. Bennett said.

Erin trembled, unable to hold in her feelings any longer. "I'll go down there now," she said, suddenly desperate to get out of the machine-driven world of Neuro-ICU. "So you and Daddy can be alone with Amy."

She followed Laurie to a very large room that looked more like a luxury hotel suite than a hospital waiting room. The carpet was dove gray, the furniture light oak wood with burgundy upholstery. "It's brand new," Laurie explained. "We've tried to make it comfortable because families like to be near each other through these crises." The lights were dim, but Erin could see people piled in oversized chairs with pillows and blankets. "Our only rule is that you can't sleep on the floor," Laurie whispered. "Local church groups bring in the food. There'll be fresh pastry and coffee here in the morning." Laurie pointed to a wall where three pay phones hung. "Give out the numbers to friends, and they can call and talk to you."

Erin realized she should call and tell Ms. Thornton something. She glanced up at a wall clock. It was three A.M. "I'll call everyone tomorrow."

Laurie gave her a skimpy pillow and a thin blue blanket and left. Erin dropped into a chair, careful not to make too much noise. She felt exhausted and numb, as if she were trapped in a bad dream and couldn't wake up. She told herself that once this terrible night was over, they'd all go back in to see Amy, and she'd be awake.

Erin consoled herself with the image of Amy sitting up in bed and eating breakfast. "Amy . . ." she pleaded in a whisper. "Please wake up, Amy. If you do, I'll be your best friend." Erin buried her face in the blanket and wept.

Throughout the remainder of the night, Erin catnapped, unable to relax in the foreign surroundings. Her parents settled near her, and she heard her mother leave often to check on Amy. Early the next morning Erin called Ms. Thornton, who promised to start the phone chain and pass along information about Amy's condition, which hadn't changed during the night. Erin also asked her to tell friends to stay away for the time being. She knew she couldn't stand visiting with a lot of people, no matter how good their intentions.

Erin called Travis, but his mother said he was asleep and promised to have him call her later. Erin hung up, realizing that, like her, he'd been up half the night and probably had slept no better than she had.

Inez came for a visit and so did a few neighbors. Shara stopped by late Sunday afternoon but didn't stay long. "Dad delivers a lot of babies at this hospital," Shara told Erin with a wave of her hand, "so I know my way around the red tape. Let me know if you want anything." Erin told her thanks but was too bewildered and overwhelmed to know what to ask for.

By afternoon the strangers in the waiting room were beginning to look familiar. Erin wondered who they all were and what patients they were waiting for, but she resisted talking to anyone. She didn't want to meet new people. She only wanted to get out of there and take Amy home.

In the light of day, Neuro-ICU didn't seem quite so formidable. The machines appeared less intimidating, and the sounds less hostile. Overhead TVs played softly despite the fact that the patients couldn't react to the programs. At the nurses' station Erin toyed with a plastic model of a human brain, tracing her fingers along the convoluted surface of the cerebrum and down to the dark mass of the cerebellum at the base of the model. She found it hard to comprehend that Amy's brain was so hurt that it had shut down.

"Fascinating isn't it?" a tall man standing beside the main desk said to her. He was dressed in a dark blue suit and had black hair and a mustache. "The average human brain weighs only three pounds, and yet it has the capacity to elevate mankind to the stars."

"Are you a doctor?" Erin asked.

"No. But I work with the staff here." His eyes were brown and kind. "Is that your sister back there?" He motioned with his head toward the glass wall.

"Yes, she was in an accident." Erin held up the plastic model. "Her brain's hurt and she's in a coma. She can't even breathe by herself."

"This unit is the best," the man said. "And the staff is tops."

Erin didn't find any comfort in his words. If everything was so medically advanced, then why didn't Amy wake up? If the human brain was so superior, then why hadn't it found a way to bring sixteen-year-old girls out of comas? She set the model down on the desk. "I'm going in to be with my sister," she told the man and walked away.

A nurse named Ellie was monitoring Amy's vital signs and making notations on a chart. Erin watched as Ellie performed several procedures. "What are you doing?" Erin asked, afraid that the nurse might try to hide something from her.

"Charting the results of her latest Glasgow test."

"What's a Glasgow test?"

Ellie showed Erin the paper with numbers neatly written in small boxes. "It's a standard for measuring a comatose patient's progress."

"Progress? But she never moves."

Ellie smiled. "Let me explain. We take temperature, pulse, and blood pressure. We check respiration—in Amy's case she's on a ventilator—and we do a few neurological tests and grade her on a scale."

"Like what?"

"For instance, we chart whether or not her eyes open. 'Spontaneously' equals a four, while 'none' equals a one." Ellie pointed to the bottom of the chart where the criteria was printed. "On 'Verbal Response'—you know, whether she reacts when you talk to her—there's a scale of one to five, with five being 'oriented' and meaning fully conscious, and one meaning 'no response.' For 'Motor Response' a five means she 'obeys commands,' and a one means 'no response.'"

She paused, and Erin examined the neat rows of charted numbers. "So where's Amy?"

"Right now she's a one-one-three."

"That's not good, is it?"

"The higher the score, the better."

"But she's a three on 'Motor Response,' Erin said hopefully.

"Yes, she reflexes to pain."

"You hurt her?"

"Not really. It's an automatic reaction of the muscles to stimuli. Like when a doctor hits your knee and it jerks. It's the way we can judge the depth of her coma and her brain-stem functions."

Erin pointed to the paper on the metal clipboard. "And what's 'Pupil Reaction' mean?"

"How well her pupils react when we shine a light

into them. Another way of gauging brain-stem functions."

Erin's head was swimming with information and starting to ache. "The numbers will go up, won't they?"

"That's what we're hoping."

Erin wanted to ask, "And what if they don't?" but lost her courage. Of course they would go up. Amy was a fighter, and their whole family was going to stand by her and help her fight.

Later she went to the cafeteria with her parents to discuss a schedule for the upcoming week. "I don't want Amy alone," Mrs. Bennett said. "When she wakes up, I want to be sure that one of us is there with her."

"I can come after classes and stay till midnight or so," Mr. Bennett said. "We'll trade off the night shift, Marian, so that every other night we each get to go home and sleep in our own bed."

"And Inez can handle the shop in the mornings, so I can stay from midnight till about ten A.M. That way I can go into the boutique at noon and stay until closing."

"Spring break starts this Thursday, so I can be up here during the days," Erin offered. "In fact, I'm positive I can get excused absences through Thursday."

"All right," Mr. Bennett said. "Erin, you and I'll go home tonight. In the morning we'll go to school, and you can get your books and assignments. I'll work my regular class schedule so that the headmaster doesn't have to find a substitute at the last minute."

"We'll need another car," Mrs. Bennett said, and Erin felt guilt sear through her like a hot iron.

"I'll rent one for us," Mr. Bennett told her. "Erin can use our station wagon."

Mrs. Bennett said nothing more about the car situation, but Erin felt her resentment. After all, if she'd driven instead of Amy, there might never have been an accident. Then another thought came to her. What if *she* had been the one in ICU instead of Amy? That idea so terrified her that she felt sick to her stomach.

What would it be like to be trapped in a coma? To be—where? Where was Amy anyway? Her body was in the room, but where were her thoughts? Did she dream? Did she think? Was it like being asleep? Or was it worse? Erin had no answers. All she had was fear. It lodged inside her heart like a monster with tentacles and began to squeeze.

Chapter Nine

The next morning Erin rode to school with her father. Outside the world seemed perfectly normal. A bright March sun made the day feel balmy, and azaleas bloomed in profusions of fuchsia, white, and pink in neighborhood yards. She wondered how everything could look so normal, so ordinary, and yet be so irreversibly changed at the same time.

"This is going to be rough on all of us," Mr. Bennett said with a deep sigh.

"We'll make it, Dad," Erin said, not at all convinced.

"According to Dr. DuPree a coma can be unpredictable. Sometimes a patient can be in one for years."

"Well, not Amy," Erin said with determination. "By the end of the week, she'll be awake and complaining."

"A physical therapist will come in soon and start exercising Amy's arms and legs to keep her muscles toned. Otherwise they can atrophy and waste away."

Erin stared out the car window and struggled for composure. It was hard to think of Amy being so silent and still. "Maybe I can learn how to exercise her and help out," she said.

"There's—uh—also the possibility of brain damage." Mr. Bennett said the phrase carefully, and Erin felt her father's eyes cut to her. "Even after she wakes up, it may take a long time for her to be all right again."

Or she may never be all right again. He hadn't said it, but Erin knew that's what he was trying to tell her. "She'll be fine, Daddy. No matter how long it takes, Amy's gonna be fine. If we all work together, she'll be just the way she was before." *Amy is only sixteen years old,* Erin thought. *She has to be all right*.

At school Erin was mobbed by concerned classmates and teachers as she collected her books and assignments. She forced herself to answer the same questions over and over, anxious to leave and go back to the hospital. She was almost out the front door when Miss Hutton hailed her.

The teacher with the high, funny voice Amy loved to imitate rushed up and said, "I'm so sorry. How could such a thing have happened to our little Amy?"

Erin gritted her teeth. Her sister wasn't Miss Hutton's "little Amy." "It was an accident," she said.

"Oh you poor dear! What a horrible, horrible ordeal for you all. And to think that this Saturday she'd planned to come with me to the Children's Home and play a clown for their big Easter party."

Erin recalled how Amy looked bobbing around her bedroom wearing the bulbous nose and floozy red wig. "She was looking forward to doing it."

"Well, when she wakes up in the hospital, you tell her not to worry about it. And you tell her that all the children will miss her terribly, but that she can come to next year's Christmas party and play the clown."

"I'll tell her."

"I'll find someone to fill in for her, but I've never had a nicer clown than Amy. And the kids are just crazy about her." Miss Hutton rested her briefcase on a nearby water fountain adding, "Before I forget . . . here's some of Amy's papers—assignments, tests, reports and such. They're graded, and I thought you might show them to her when she's recovering. The grades are good, so they might cheer her up." The older woman smiled broadly and handed over a sheaf of papers.

Erin mumbled "Thanks," and shoved them into her duffel bag, then left the school pondering Miss Hutton's words. She'd often thought of Amy as "scatterbrained" and "silly," as a show-off who could never say no. But she realized how warm and giving Amy was too. Erin told herself that she had much to share with her sister when she came out of her coma—and a lot to make up for.

At the hospital Erin relieved her mother, who looked about ready to drop. "You call me at home if there's *any* change," Mrs. Bennett told her before leaving. Erin promised, then settled in for the long afternoon vigil.

In the sun-filled waiting room Erin recognized a

few faces from the night before, but she kept to herself, too tired to socialize or make friends. She snuggled into a chair. A television soap opera droned in the background. The chair felt soft and cozy. Erin's eyelids drooped, and her head nodded downward.

She dreamed that she and Amy were unwrapping gifts, but Amy had a long hose attached to her mouth, and she couldn't laugh. Erin tried to reach over and pull the tube out, but her hand kept knocking against an invisible glass wall, and no matter how hard she tried, she couldn't get through it.

The warmth of the dream gave way to anxiety, and Erin's heart began to pound. She reached out toward her sister, who kept busy and was oblivious to her. She heard someone calling her name. From far away the voice beckoned, "Wake up, Erin. Wake up."

She jumped, suddenly awake, and found her arms wrapped around Travis's neck.

Confused, and then extremely embarrassed, Erin let go of Travis and pressed hard into the back of the chair. She mumbled his name, still trying to separate the dream from reality. What was he doing here in the middle of a school day?

"Are you all right?" he asked.

"I think so." Her face burned. "I–I guess I fell asleep."

He rose from his crouched position and dropped into the chair next to her. "You look tired."

"What time is it?"

He looked up at the wall clock. "One o'clock. I—uh—didn't go to school today. I called the hospital, but they only said Amy was in fair condition, so I decided to drive over and check things out. What's happening?"

"There's no change. She's still in a coma. My folks and I are taking turns staying round the clock until Amy wakes up."

"How long will it take?"

"The doctors don't know."

Travis's expression fell. "That stinks."

Erin shifted and straightened out her leg, which had cramped. She got a sudden idea. "Would you like to go in and see her?"

"I—uh—I thought only family could go inside."

"They'll let you in if I ask them."

He looked hesitant and wary. "Gee, Erin, I don't know. . . ."

She wanted him to come with her. Somehow she felt she owed it to Amy because Amy cared about him so much. "Please, Travis. When she's better, she'll ask if you came. You know how Amy can be if she thinks someone isn't thinking about her one hundred percent of the time."

"I'll never hear the end of it," he said, his smile softening the look of panic on his face. "After I took you to the concert and after I told her the details, all she asked was, 'Did you miss me?' As if I thought about anything else all night."

His confession stung Erin, making her realize how one-sided her feelings for him really were. She stood up. "Come on, Travis, come see Amy with me. Talk to her. The nurses said that it's important to talk to people in comas. They told me that patients often wake up and tell them that even though they couldn't respond, they remember hearing someone talking to them and encouraging them."

He hesitated but followed her down the hall. At the closed door of ICU, Erin explained the situation through a speaker in the wall to Becky, the daytime nurse. They were admitted, and Erin continued to lead him through the unit toward the partitioned area where Amy lay.

Amy's body was motionless, but Becky approached and announced cheerfully, "You've got visitors, Amy. It's your sister and a friend named Travis." Becky patted Amy's arm. The ventilator hissed, and Amy's chest rose up and down under the white sheet. Dark bruising had appeared around her eye sockets, and her coloring seemed ashen, not pink and glowing.

Erin stroked Amy's cheek. "Travis is with me, Ames. And when I stopped by school to get my books, everyone there asked about you. Even Miss Hutton." Erin felt as if she were talking to a doll. She glanced toward Travis, who had backed up all the way to the wall, his expression wooden. "Do you want to tell Amy anything?" she asked.

"No." He looked cornered, trapped. "I want to go now."

"But you've hardly seen her," Erin protested.

"I've seen her enough."

Becky stepped forward and told Erin, "Perhaps you could come back later."

Travis brushed around them and hurried to the door. "I'll see you outside, Erin."

He was gone, and Erin faced the nurse over Amy's bed. "I–I guess it was getting to him," she apologized.

"It's not unusual."

"I'd better go check on him."

Becky nodded, and Erin took one last lingering look at her sister and said, "I'll be back later, Ames, all right?" She felt a little foolish asking permission, because Amy couldn't answer. Erin turned quickly and left ICU to look for Travis.

She found him back in the waiting room taking long gulps from a can of cola. "Are you okay?" she asked.

"Sure." He shrugged and looked sheepish. "It was tougher than I thought, seeing her that way."

"She's going to be fine," Erin said. "It's gonna take some time, that's all."

Travis shifted nervously. "Listen, I bought her a stuffed animal, but I left it down in my car. Can I bring it over to your house later? Maybe you could bring it up to her, and she could have it in her room. Do you think that'll be all right with the nurses?"

Erin considered his plea. He'd bought Amy a gift, which was more than she had done. And maybe it would be a good idea to bring some of Amy's familiar things from home so that when she woke up, she'd see them and not be scared. "How about tonight? I'll be home after supper."

"I'll see you later," Travis said, and after he'd gone, she stared at the floor where he'd stood until her legs ached.

Erin ate a quick supper in the hospital cafeteria and returned to the waiting room only to see her mother sitting alone in a corner and smoking a cigarette.

"Are you relieving me, Mom?" she asked, feeling awkward.

Mrs. Bennett casually snuffed out the cigarette and said, "Don't look so disapproving, Erin. It settles my nerves, and it's better than taking tranquilizers."

"You don't have to explain it to me." The room was nearly deserted, and Erin assumed that the "regulars" were at supper and would be returning soon. "Travis came up today," she said. "But he didn't handle it too well."

"I'm not surprised. Dr. DuPree said he'll have another CAT scan run tomorrow. There's still a lot of intracranial pressure." Mrs. Bennett took out another cigarette and lit it.

"What's that mean?"

"It means that if her brain continues to swell, he'll have to operate to relieve the pressure."

The word "operate" made Erin's stomach lurch. "That sounds scary."

Mrs. Bennett tapped the ash off the end of her cigarette. "There's something else you need to be aware of, Erin. It happened this afternoon and gave me a lot of false hope."

"What?"

"Amy moved."

Erin gasped audibly. "You mean she might be coming out of the coma?"

Mrs. Bennett shook her head impatiently. "No, that's not it at all. I thought it was, but when I ran for the nurse, she explained to me that what I saw was simple spinal reflex. Nothing more. You know, like a knee jerking when it's hit in the right spot. So if you see her hand move, or her eyelids flutter, that's all it probably is."

Erin realized how much her mother's hopes had been dashed by the medical explanation of Amy's movement and wished she could take away her disappointment. "Thanks for warning me," she said.

Her mother blinked hard and crossed her arms. "I don't want Amy to be a vegetable, Erin. I don't want her hooked to machines for the rest of her life, unable to talk or smile ever again."

"That's not going to happen to Amy," Erin said fiercely. "The quality of Amy's life is important," Mrs. Bennett continued. "She's too young to live the rest of her life in a nursing home."

"That's not going—"

"Stop it, Erin!" her mother interrupted. "Of course it can happen to Amy. That's the bottom line when she comes out of her coma. *If* she comes out of it."

Erin wanted to clamp her hands over her ears. How could her mother be saying those things? How could she even suggest the hideous alternative to being kept alive by machines? She felt a growing pressure at the base of her skull and knew that a headache was coming on. "M–mom, please don't give up on Amy."

Mrs. Bennett reached out and tucked Erin's hair over her shoulder. "Is that what you think I'm doing? I'm not giving up. I'm just tired, and I feel so helpless whenever I go in there and see her lying so still."

"But she's *alive*," Erin said. "And that's what counts."

Her mother ground out her cigarette and stood. "Go on home, Erin. Wake your father at ten so that he can come down here and stay with Amy and me. I'll be home later."

Erin watched her mother head down to ICU, feeling as if her insides were being torn out. Why was this happening to their family? Why had she let Amy talk her into driving the car? If only she could turn back the hands of the clock.

"Are you all right?" The voice caused Erin to jump, and she turned to face a girl her own age with dark hair and wide gray eyes. "Sorry, I didn't mean to scare you," the girl said. "I'm Beth Clark, and I saw you come in the other night."

Erin mumbled a self-conscious greeting and wished Beth would go away.

"Why are you here?" Beth asked.

Erin told her, then realized that it was only fair to ask, "And why are you here?"

Beth stared off in the distance. "It's my mother." Her gaze found Erin's again. "She's dying, and her only hope is if somebody else dies before she does."

Chapter Ten

"I don't understand," Erin said to Beth, taken aback by her extraordinary statement.

"My mom's had kidney disease for years. This past year she's gotten worse, so they put her on dialysis three days a week. She was an outpatient, so I dropped her off for treatments on my way to school and picked her up on my way home from school."

"I've heard about dialysis," Erin said slowly.

"It's being hooked up to a machine that does the work of the kidneys." Beth explained. "The machine cleans the blood, and each exchange takes about six hours."

Another machine doing the work of a human organ, Erin thought. "Let's hear it for technology," she said without sarcasm.

Beth sank into an upholstered chair, and Erin took the chair next to her. "Anyway, dialysis helps, but it's no way to spend the rest of your life. I've got a brother and two sisters, and we'd like to have Mom well."

"So what now?"

"She needs a kidney transplant. We've been waiting for a donor for months."

"Is that why she's here?"

"Not really. She got sick, so they checked her into the hospital, but she's getting better."

Erin found herself keenly interested. She'd read about kidney and heart transplants, and now here was a real-live person who needed one. "How will they find a donor?"

Beth toyed with a silver necklace. "Oh, she's been programmed into a computer bank. That way if someone dies and donates his organs, doctors can check for compatibility. You know, a good match of tissues so her body won't reject the new kidney. At home we're always on call. Everytime the phone rings, it could be the hospital saying they've found a donor. If that happens, we drop everything and go for the transplant."

"And if they don't find one?"

"They'll send her home again without one. This time they're putting a portable dialysis machine in our house, and she'll be almost one hundred percent bed-ridden. Our lives would be so much easier if they could find a kidney for her."

Erin saw sadness in Beth's eyes, and she felt sorry for her. But she saw the unfairness of the situation too. Finding Beth's mother a kidney meant that someone, someplace, had to die. The idea made her shudder. She didn't quite know what to say, so she changed the subject and asked about Beth's school.

It turned out that she was a junior at a huge public high school. She had a boyfriend—"the tall guy with red hair who sits in the corner with me during the evenings." Erin remembered seeing him.

Beth asked, "Was that boy who was here earlier your boyfriend? I saw you hugging him."

Erin reddened. "No, Travis is my sister's boy-friend. I was having a bad dream, and he woke me up, and I just grabbed him."

"He's cute."

"Yeah, well, he and Amy have been hot and heavy since before Christmas."

"Is that your sister's name? Amy?"

Erin nodded but found herself reluctant to dis-cuss her sister's situation. She quickly looked up at the clock and said, "Gee, Beth, I've got to be going. Travis is stopping by my house sometime tonight, and I don't want him to wake my dad. We're all taking shifts, and it's Dad's turn to spend the night."

"No problem. I wanted to say hi to you sooner, but you kind of looked like you wanted to be left alone."

"I didn't mean to be antisocial, but it's been a tough few days. Some of the other people in here have tried to get a conversation going, but I just didn't feel up to it."

"Hey, that's okay, I understand. It's crazy. You spend night and day with these strangers, and the only thing you have in common is that somebody is really sick, maybe dying, and you sort of band to-gether for support. When they leave, you never see them again, but while you're here, together in this room, they're the best friends you have."

"You sound like the voice of experience."

Beth gave a wry smile. "Five times in the past fourteen months I've camped in this place. I sure hope they find a kidney for my mom soon. I feel like a hospital groupie."

Erin laughed and gathered her things. She promised Beth she'd see her the next day and headed for the elevator. Erin was halfway down before she realized that it was the first time she'd laughed in the past three days, it had felt good.

Erin let herself into her house and shivered. The silence was eerie. No lamps were lit, and the rooms were dark and chilly. She found a note from her dad saying he couldn't sleep and had gone to the library, and that he'd be home by ten to get ready to go to the hospital.

Erin deposited her things in her room, took a hot shower, washed her hair, and began to blow-dry it. She'd never felt so drained and sapped in her life, not even after a grueling dance performance. She stared at the mirror thoughtfully. She hadn't thought about dancing in days. There'd been a time when that was all she thought about. Funny how the focus of your life can shift so drastically.

Her fine blond hair danced about her head as the dryer worked. Terpsicord, Ms. Thornton, and Wolftrap seemed light-years away. She'd never even told Amy about Wolftrap. She'd been upset with her and had perversely held back the news. Yet Erin knew that if she *had* said something, Amy's response would have been totally excited and encouraging.

A lump rose in Erin's throat. There were so many things she wanted to say to her sister, so many times she'd growled at her or teased her that she wanted to take back. If only Amy would wake up, Erin swore she'd never be mean to her again.

Listlessly Erin finished dressing and wandered to the living room. She put on a cassette of Amy's favorite rock group and pulled out the stack of family photo albums. Her mother had kept them up-to-date, and Erin started with the one that featured Amy's birth. She'd just gotten past the photos of an infant Amy in the hospital nursery when the doorbell rang. Travis stood on the doorstep. She brought him into the living room and plopped onto the floor.

"I was just going through some old pictures," she explained.

He tossed the stuffed bear he was carrying onto the sofa and sat down beside her. "Amy?" he asked, pointing to a dark-haired toddler, holding two fistfuls of birthday cake.

"She was a terror," Erin said with a wistful smile.

"Is this you?" He indicated one of a six-year-old Erin dressed in a tutu with her arms poised over her head.

She made a face at her roly-poly image. "That was taken before my very first recital. Look at all that baby fat."

"There's no baby fat on you now," Travis said, and

his observation made her stomach feel fluttery. He was sitting so close that she caught his fresh, clean scent.

They flipped through the albums and watched the years parade past in a collection of color photos. Amy in her playpen. Erin on her first tricycle. Amy with her front teeth missing and clutching her school lunch box. Erin wearing a crown as May Day queen in the fifth grade.

"When was this one taken?" Travis asked.

Erin gazed at a blowup of one of her father's favorite photographs. Erin and Amy were running barefoot through a grassy field full of dandelions, their long hair streaming behind them, their mouths wide with laughter.

"I still remember that day," Erin said. "I was five and Amy had just turned four. I thought that field was the most beautiful thing I'd ever seen, that it was a place where a fairy princess lived. And all Amy wanted to do was run around and make the seeds fly off the weeds. I started to cry and asked Dad to make Amy stop, but of course she didn't, and I eventually got into the game too. We chased those seeds for over an hour. I can still see them floating away in the sky."

They stared at the photo in silence until a wave of melancholia engulfed her and she was afraid she might start crying. She looked at Travis, and his expression was blank. She wondered what he was thinking, and then she saw the cuddly stuffed bear on the sofa. "Is that for Amy?"

Travis followed her line of vision. "Yeah. She saw

it at the mall and made a big fuss about how cute it was. So I bought it for her."

"I asked the nurses if it was all right to bring some of her things from home for her room, and they said I could. Why don't you just bring the bear up to her tomorrow?"

Travis studied the bear for a long moment before speaking. "I'm not going back up there, Erin."

"What?"

"Not until Amy's sitting up in her bed and talking."

"But it may help her subconsciously knowing that you're in the room with her."

He looked at Erin as if she were crazy. "Erin, she doesn't know when *anyone's* in the room with her."

Erin snapped, "How do you know? What makes you an authority?"

"Take it easy," Travis said with a placating tone. "I'll keep calling for reports, and you can call me too. But I can't go back inside that room when she's so—you know—so out of it."

"She's unconscious. She'll wake up."

"She's in a coma. It's different."

By now they were both on their feet amid the jumble of photo albums. "It's just a deep sleep, that's all. It's a way for her brain to recover from being so banged around."

"Erin, face reality. She can't even *breathe* by herself."

Erin wanted to scream at him, but just then her father came home. "Is something wrong?" he asked.

Erin stood facing Travis, her heart pounding, her fists balled. "Travis was just leaving," she said tersely.

Travis mumbled apologetic words to Erin and her dad and retreated out the door. She longed to slam it hard against his back.

"What was *that* all about?" Mr. Bennett asked when she bent and started piling the albums.

"Nothing. He's just so negative about Amy's condition, and I got mad. He says he's not even going up to see her again until she comes out of the coma."

Mr. Bennett knelt down next to her and held her by the shoulders. "Don't be so upset about it, honey."

Erin felt tears well up in her eyes. "But she likes him so much, and he acts like he doesn't even care!"

"You can't expect everyone to handle this thing in the same way, Erin. Grief doesn't affect us all alike."

"Grief?" She said the word incredulously. "Grief is when you cry. Travis isn't crying. I guess he's too macho for tears."

"In other words, real men don't cry?"

She held her spine stiff and put a chill in her voice. "Real men stick by the people they say they care about. They don't have to bawl and blubber, but they *do* have to keep their promises. And Travis Sinclair told me he really liked Amy. Now he's not even going to go see her in the hospital."

She thought of all the fantasies she'd had about him, of how much she'd longed to have him as a boyfriend, and felt even more betrayed. "He's acting like a creep, Daddy. A genuine creep!"

Chapter Eleven

"Don't judge him too harshly," Mr. Bennett said. "There's more to grieving than crying. And there's more to caring than hovering over someone's bedside."

The lamplight glowed on the side of his face, and for the first time Erin noticed the bags under his eyes and lines around his mouth. He had a whole night ahead of him to spend in the hospital, and here she was taking out her anger at Travis on her father. "I'm sorry, I didn't mean to get so upset."

Mr. Bennett smiled pensively. "That's okay, honey, we're all on edge these days." He picked up an album and leafed through the plastic-covered pages. "I remember when she was just learning to talk, and your mom and I would ask, 'What does your sister want, Erin?' And you'd tell us, and sure enough, that's what it was. You two always seemed to understand each other. I think underneath you're very much alike, even though on the outside you have different styles."

He rose, crossed to the buffet, and rummaged through the junk drawer. "I got the birthday pictures back a week ago and tossed them in here for your mother to put in the album." He withdrew the packet and brought it over to Erin. "They turned out good, huh?"

Erin sorted through them—Amy grinning from behind her birthday cake, Amy holding up the car keys and special key chain Erin had given her. A lump wedged in Erin's throat. Could it have been only a few weeks ago that they were all so happy and carefree? "Yeah, Dad, they're super." She placed them carefully inside the back cover of an album.

"Maybe when this is all over, you mom will put them in order," he said. "Maybe this will be the birthday we remember most of all."

"Amy will wake up, won't she, Dad?" Erin hadn't wanted to ask the question but couldn't help herself. Her conversation with her mother earlier still weighed on her mind.

"The doctors aren't making any promises."

"If she doesn't, will we have to put her in a nursing home?" The idea made Erin shiver.

"What do you suppose Amy would want?"

"She'd want to come home."

"How would we care for her?"

"We could." Erin jutted her chin stubbornly. "Between the three of us, we could take care of her."

Mr. Bennett eased onto the sofa. He picked up the bear and stroked its fur. "The doctor asked us about putting a 'Do not resuscitate' order on Amy's chart this morning."

"Meaning what?"

"Meaning that should her heart stop suddenly, they wouldn't do anything to start it beating again."

Erin stared at him blankly as his words sunk in. The house was so silent that she heard the ticking of the hall clock. "You mean, let her die?"

Mr. Bennett kept studying the teddy bear. "She's going to have massive brain damage, Erin. She'll never be normal."

"But they can't just let her *die*. Please, Daddy, don't let them do that. They have to start her heart."

He turned anguished eyes on her. "Honey, Erin. Take it easy . . . it's all right. Her heart's very strong right now, so don't worry."

Erin had gone cold all over. She dug her nails into her palms, hoping the instant pain would keep her from screaming. "How could her doctors suggest such a thing? Aren't they supposed to do everything to keep a person alive?"

Mr. Bennett let out a deep, weary sigh and rubbed his hand over his forehead. "They are, Erin. But lately I've wondered, What's the distinction between prolonging life and postponing death? Can't you see the difference between the two?"

"What about, 'Thou shall not kill'?" Erin grabbed at the commandment as if it were a lifeline. "If they let her die, it's the same as killing her."

"But if they didn't have the machines in the first place, wouldn't Amy have died already? There's a saying that everything under the sun has a season, that there's 'a time to live and a time to die.' What about

Amy's time to die, Erin? What right does medicine have to tamper this way with her season?"

Erin was afraid she was going to be sick. Her father's questions were frightening her. She had never thought about such things before, and she couldn't think about them now. Especially about Amy. "But you said her heart's fine, didn't you?"

"Yes, honey, she's young and strong. They were only asking what we'd want done should she suddenly die, that's all. We live in a world where technology gives us options. They can restart her heart"—he paused and cleared his throat—"or they can let her go."

Erin pressed her lips together. "Well, I want them to start her heart again if it should stop. So that's my choice. What do you and Mom want to do?"

"The same thing."

Erin sagged and let out her breath. "I guess it's real complicated, isn't it?"

"It's very complicated. If Amy never comes out of her coma, we're probably dooming her to a life in an institution."

"But she may wake up," Erin countered, her voice quavering. "The machines are helping her live long enough for her brain to get better. That's the way I see it."

Mr. Bennett stroked the teddy bear's tummy. Erin wanted to throw herself in her father's arms, but she was too old for that. Too old to cry like a baby. "Thanks for talking to me, Dad. I–I'm glad you told me what the doctors asked."

"We're a family, Erin. Your wishes count too." He stood, smoothed his rumpled shirt, and plunked the stuffed bear on the couch. He said, "I'd better get ready and get down to the hospital so your mother can come home and get some sleep."

"Sure." Erin began to gather the photo albums, spread out in a jumble around her. "I'm going to clean up here and go to bed." He left the room, and Erin shut each book, being very careful not to look at any more pictures.

When she was finished, she picked up the teddy bear and hugged it to her breasts. It smelled new but also carried the sweet, pungent aroma of her father's pipe tobacco. She cuddled it tenderly and rocked back and forth on her knees until she heard her father leave for the hospital.

By Wednesday Erin had settled into a routine of relieving her mother midmorning and staying until one of her parents relieved her in the early evening. The monotony of the day was broken by Beth, who came straight from school every afternoon.

"I'm glad Easter break starts tomorrow," Beth told Erin as she nibbled on a handful of potato chips.

"Me too," Erin said, thinking of the plans she'd made a month before with Shara to go to the beach and stare at the college guys down from the northern campuses. There'd be no sun-filled vacation for her now.

She and Beth started a game of Monopoly. "How's your sister today?"

"The CAT they just did didn't show any more swelling, so at least they won't have to operate."

"That's good."

"But it didn't show the doctors anything else promising," Erin countered. "They'll do another one in a few days."

"Did you put the things in her room like you told me you were going to do?"

"Only some stuffed animals, but I want to put up her life-size poster of Tom Cruise on one of the walls tonight. The nurses didn't seem to mind when I asked if it was okay."

"Who would mind?" Beth joked. "At least when she comes out of her coma, there'll be something worth waking up for."

"Right," Erin agreed. "Whenever she comes out of her coma."

That evening at home Erin went into Amy's bedroom to take down the poster. She entered hesitantly momentarily surprised. The room was spotless, neat and orderly. Clothes had been hung up, papers stacked, pillows arranged on the tidily made up coverlet. It didn't look like Amy's room at all. "Inez . . ." she muttered. Hadn't her mother told her that one of Inez's friends was coming over to clean their house? Obviously, she'd come.

Erin walked around the room. It was too quiet and seemed foreign to her. Without Amy, Erin could scarcely stand to be in it. She stopped at Amy's dresser and fingered a pile of papers. She wondered if Amy would have to learn to read all over again. She'd seen a television report once about people who'd had brain damage and they'd had to relearn certain things as if they were babies. "I'll help you, Amy," she vowed, rearranging the pile.

She scanned the photographs stuck into the wooden frame around the mirror. Travis and Amy smiled out at her. She stared hard at his handsome face. He'd kept his promise and called once a day for an update, but Erin was cool to him. How could he refuse to come see her sister? She wondered what he'd be doing over spring break.

Erin turned toward the poster of Tom Cruise and spied Amy's makeup kit in the corner. She lifted it onto the bed and opened the lid. Tubes of greasepaint were scattered inside. The fuzzy red wig and the bright red nose were also there. False eyelashes and a pair of oversize rubber ears were wrapped in wads of tissue.

Erin went to the closet and dug around until she found the satin clown suit and floppy shoe coverings that extended outward a foot long. On the same hanger with the costume was a stiff white net bib with sequins. She ran her hand over the smooth satin. On Saturday Amy was to have appeared at the Children's Home. Erin wondered what the kids would be told. She wondered if they'd ask Miss Hutton, "But where's Amy?"

Unexpected tears welled up in Erin's eyes as she thought about the children. Why should she feel so sad about it? Why should she care? Amy couldn't be there, and that's the way it was. *But you can,* she thought, startled.

"I don't know anything about being a clown," she argued aloud.

You can go in Amy's place, the voice inside said.

"But I'll feel so stupid dressed this way."

It's for Amy. And the kids.

"This is the dumbest idea you've ever had, Erin Bennett," she announced. Yet even as she said it, Erin knew she was going to go find her father's Briarwood faculty phone directory and call Miss Hutton and volunteer.

Quickly she gathered up the costume and the makeup kit and hurried from the bedroom. Her pulse was racing, excitement carrying her down the hallway. She had something to do. Something to give to the kids at the Children's Home, and no matter how silly and foolish she felt about being a clown, she'd do it. For Amy.

Chapter Twelve

Erin hid in the rest room at the Children's Home until the last possible moment. A glance in the mirror told her all she wanted to know about how she looked dressed as a clown. She looked ridiculous. Yet she was experiencing some sense of satisfaction in the achievement. When she'd called Miss Hutton, the teacher had been so delighted that she'd personally driven Erin to the Home, chattering and complimenting her all the way.

"This is so wonderful of you, Erin," Miss Hutton had said in her distinctive, high-pitched voice. "I did manage to find someone to fill in for Amy—a young man from Berkshire Prep named David. You'll meet him at the Home. But the more clowns the merrier, I always say." Erin only nodded and mumbled.

Miss Hutton barreled ahead. "The party will start in the activity room, then move out to the lawn where the staff has hidden about one hundred Easter eggs. I know you don't have much experience in this sort of thing, but the children are so fascinated by clowns that they won't notice. Most are five to ten years old, and they're so adorable."

Once at the facility Erin had retreated to the

bathroom to begin her transformation. She'd watched Amy several times and felt she could reconstruct her sister's clown from memory. First she applied a base coat of white greasepaint. Next she filled in a wide mouth of bright red well beyond the perimeters of her own lips and drew large red circles on her cheeks. She pasted on the false eyelashes and drew eyebrows that arched high on her forehead. The red wig and bulbous nose topped off her appearance. In many ways she looked like Amy, but the resemblance so disconcerted her that she drew a row of bright blue tears from the corner of one eye to the edge of her jaw.

She donned the satin costume, tied the bib behind her neck, and slipped the floppy rubber shoes over her sneakers. "Good grief, it's like trying to walk in swim flippers," she said, taking a few cautious steps.

Yet she *had* become a clown to rival any that performed in the circus, and she was sure that Amy would be proud of her. She announced, "Well, here goes nothing," took a deep breath, and edged out the door. One of the outsize rubber shoes got stuck in the doorway. "Drat!" she muttered, and struggled to pull it free.

"Need some help?" someone asked.

Erin jerked upright, only to have the shoe slip free and the door swing shut. She toppled backward and landed in the arms of another clown.

"Do you always throw yourself at guys this way?" he asked with a laugh, hauling her to her feet.

She felt totally embarrassed, then realized that he

couldn't see her blush because of all her makeup. "That wasn't funny," she said, squaring her shoulders. Even though he was wearing full makeup, she saw mischief sparkling in his blue eyes, and she thought of how silly she must look trying to act dignified in a clown face and outfit. Erin started to giggle.

The boy's face, already painted with a lopsided grin, smiled more broadly. "Hi, I'm David, fellow clown and court jester. You must be Amy."

Erin sobered quickly. "No, I'm Amy's sister. I'm filling in for her. She's"—Erin searched for an explanation—"sick."

"Too bad. I've heard she was terrific, and I was looking forward to working with her."

"You do this often?"

"Every chance I get. I have a magic act too, but my specialty is balloons."

"Balloons?"

"Yeah, I make animals and things for the kids out of balloons. Let me show you." He reached into the pocket of the billowing overcoat he wore, pulled out a balloon, and proceeded to blow it up.

Erin watched, fascinated, as he puffed and twisted and shaped the pliant elongated balloon. A minute later he held out a giraffe. "That's super," she said, taking it. "How do you do that?"

"Trade secret," he whispered. "What's your specialty?"

Suddenly Erin realized that she couldn't *do* anything. How had Amy managed these appearances?

What had she done to entertain her audience? "I–I don't know. Like I said, this is my sister's gig."

David pondered her, tapping his fat clown shoe on the polished tile floor. The makeup around his mouth turned into a sad-sack frown. "You need a gimmick," he said. "Here, take my water flower, and every chance you get, squirt me in the face."

"Oh, but I couldn't. . . ." She backed away, but he whipped off the large plastic daisy from his lapel. A long thin hose led from the back of the flower to a bulb.

"You feed the hose down your sleeve and keep the bulb in your palm." He explained how the gizmo worked as he pinned it on her costume and pushed the tubing inside her sleeve along her arm.

Erin was amazed by his brashness but soon realized that he didn't think of her as anything but a fellow clown out for the biggest laugh. Just the way Amy would have acted. "Uh—thanks," she mumbled when he had finished.

"Try it." She squeezed the bulb, and a spout of water doused him in the face. "Outstanding," he said. "So, this is your first gig?"

"Yes. My last too," she added yanking at the constricting bib around her throat. "If I don't choke to death before the end of the day."

"Want to work up a little routine?"

"Like what?"

"The kids like it when you do pratfalls."

Erin looked skeptical, thinking of her dance aspirations. She didn't want to hurt herself. "Gee, I don't know. . . ."

"I'll do all the falling," David assured her. "You just trip me up."

"Are you sure?"

"Positive. I do this stuff all the time. I won't feel a thing."

Erin agreed, and they did a few practice moves. Each time David sprawled convincingly on the floor. Finally satisfied, he rose, dusted himself off, and offered his arm in courtly fashion. "Shall we adjourn to the activity room?"

Erin hooked her arm through his and curtsied. "Lead on, fool." They started down the hall, each lifting oversize rubber feet in cautious, exaggerated steps, being careful not to trip one another.

The activity room was packed with small kids and personnel, and in no time David had won their hearts with his antics and balloon creatures.

Erin followed his cues and tripped him often. She sneaked behind him and tapped him on the shoulder. The kids shouted warnings, but he turned and took a faceful of water. No matter how predictable her action was, the children squealed in delight. Behind the anonymity of the makeup, she was able to act with outrageous abandon.

When the staff director announced the start of the egg hunt, Erin was almost sorry. David helped form a line and led the children out into the sunshine. Erin didn't follow but hung behind. Without the shouts of the audience, the room seemed hollow, and she watched from the window for a few moments, then let out a sigh. For her the party was over.

"There you are, Erin," Miss Hutton said, coming in from the bright outdoors. "You were wonderful, dear. The children are asking for you. Won't you come help find the eggs with them?"

"I really need to get back to the hospital," she explained.

Miss Hutton's expression turned to instant understanding. "Well, of course you do. Let me get my purse and drive you home."

Erin watched David prancing on the lawn with a dark-haired girl who kept dodging him and laughing. An overwhelming sadness descended on her. "Thanks. I'll need to clean up before I go."

Miss Hutton touched her arm. "The children will long remember this day, Erin. Thank you for coming."

"I did it for Amy."

"You charmed everyone. So did that young man, David."

"Miss Hutton, if he asks about me, don't tell him who I am or where I've gone. I'd like him and the children to remember me as just a clown."

"If that's what you want."

It was what Erin wanted—to be associated with laughter. She took off the floppy shoes so that she could walk more quickly and started for the door. Her foot brushed against an inflated balloon, and it danced upward in the air. She caught it and held it up. It was tied off in the middle to form a heart, and she decided to keep it as a souvenir.

David was very talented, and he had the gift of laughter. Too bad she'd never see him again. She wondered what he really looked like, then decided she didn't really want to know. This day had merely been an interlude in time, a brief time-out from all the pain and turmoil in her real life. She tucked the heart-shaped balloon under her arm and hurried down the hall to gather her things and make a quick escape.

On Easter Sunday, Erin went to a small chapel service in the hospital. It felt strange not to dress in new spring clothes and go to church with her family, where the choir would sing Handel's *Messiah* and baskets of white lilies would line the altar and aisles. This year the Bennetts would be sitting in Neuro-ICU instead of in the sanctuary.

They ate Easter dinner in the cafeteria, but there was no sense of joy in the meal. "They'll do another CAT scan tomorrow," Mrs. Bennett said, pushing aside her half-eaten food.

"You should eat more, Marian," Mr. Bennett told her.

"How can I eat? How can I even think about eating when my baby's upstairs attached to wires and machines?"

Erin's eyes darted quickly between her parents. *Don't let there be a scene,* she pleaded silently.

"Well, how's starving yourself going to help Amy?" he argued. "I'll bet you've lost ten pounds."

"So what? I'd lose a hundred if I thought it would help her." She reached in her purse for a cigarette.

"Well it won't."

Erin scraped back her chair and flung her napkin over her plate. "Stop it! Just stop it! It's Easter Sunday. And . . . and . . ." Her voice broke. She wanted to scream at them, wanted them to understand how bad she felt and how much she wished she could turn time backward. "I'm going up to the waiting room," Erin cried, and fled to the stairwell. She bolted up the stairs, two at a time, and by the fifth-floor landing she could scarcely breathe. Somehow she made it to the seventh-floor landing, where she stood gasping for air, sweat trickling down her face and back.

Her legs felt rubbery, but she pushed through the stairwell door and let it slam shut. She had almost regained her composure by the time she reached the waiting room, and the moment she entered, she sensed an air of expectancy.

Beth rushed over to her, her eyes shining with exuberance. "I'm so glad you came! I was afraid I'd miss you."

"What's happened? Is it your mom? Is she going home?"

"Better," Beth said, her voice breathy. "They found her a donor kidney, and we're on our way to Gainesville for the transplant operation."

Chapter Thirteen

"You're leaving?"

"As soon as possible. The donor's on a ventilator. He was in a motorcycle accident and was declared brain dead real early this morning. His family decided to donate his organs, and my mom was matched by the computer."

"But why do you have to go to Gainesville for the surgery?"

"There's a transplant team waiting and ready to go at the University of Florida's School of Medicine. The man's other organs will be flown to other hospitals for transplantation, but Mom's well enough to travel, so we're flying there."

An absurd picture from a Frankenstein movie flashed into Erin's mind—the mad scientist robbing graves to give his creature life. Beth's news seemed so farfetched, but the look of joy on her face told Erin that it was happening for real. "I'm glad for you—for your whole family. What did they tell you about the donor?"

"Oh, they never tell you much. All we know is that he was twenty-three and healthy. And that his kidney is compatible." Erin nodded. It was true that he'd have no use for his organs now. Perhaps it was best that they could go to help someone else live. And without a new kidney, Beth's mom was pretty much doomed. Erin reached out and squeezed Beth's hands. "We didn't know each other very long, but I feel very close to you."

Beth gave an understanding smile. "It's the waiting-room syndrome I told you about. Life and death get people together real quick."

"It turns complete strangers into buddies, right?"

"Erin, I don't even know that boy's family in Gainesville, but I love them. I love them because they're saving my mom's life."

A film of tears formed in Erin's eyes. "How long before you come home?"

"About a month if everything goes perfect." Beth had once told Erin that there were no guarantees that the kidney would function properly once it was transplanted, but that the risk was worth taking. She wondered if she'd still be sitting in the hospital waiting room in a month. "You have my home number, don't you?"

"I'll keep in touch," Beth promised. Someone called to her. "I gotta go." She ran a few steps, then stopped and turned. "I hope Amy gets well, Erin. I hope she wakes up and goes home real soon."

Erin watched her leave and felt a hole opening up inside her. She would miss Beth. She glanced around the waiting area and for the first time realized that she was an "old-timer" in the room. The others had come and gone as their relatives had recovered. She sniffed and wondered how much longer she and her parents could live in this limbo. Then Erin remembered that it was Easter Sunday, and that made it especially fitting for Beth's mom to receive a second chance at life. After all, wasn't resurrection supposed to follow death?

Monday's CAT scan on Amy showed no improvement, and her Glasgow tests had lowered to a one-one-two status. Her eyes weren't opened, she didn't respond to verbal commands, and her motor response to pain had diminished.

On Wednesday Erin's parents decided that they should all try to resume a more normal schedule. "The hospital will contact us if there's any change," Mrs. Bennett said when Erin argued that she wanted to stay during the day instead of returning to school.

"It makes no sense for us to just hang around here day after day this way," Mrs. Bennett insisted. "It's killing me."

Mr. Bennett agreed. "Work is good for us, Erin. It'll keep our minds occupied. And if they call us, we'll be at Briarwood together so we can come here together."

Erin returned to school on Thursday, sullen and angry with her parents. Her classmates and teachers greeted and hugged her, and by noon even she had to admit that she was better off at school than sitting around the waiting room.

"We missed you over break," Shara told her at lunch. "I went to the beach with Kori and Donna, and we met some guys from Northwestern." She bobbed her eyebrows lecherously. "We were naughty but nice. I dated two of them at the same time."

Erin listened to Shara's tales with a twinge of envy. She felt as if she were caught in a time warp and wondered if her life would ever be back to normal. "I don't think that's what the term 'double dating' means, Shara."

Her friend laughed and said, "Spring Fling's Saturday night. I invited Kenny after all. I guess you won't be going, huh?"

Erin had forgotten all about the dance until that moment. She recalled how much Amy had wanted to go with Travis, and how she'd felt sorry for herself because she'd had no one special in her life to even think about asking. "I don't think I'd have much fun."

"Lots of girls will be there without dates," Shara ventured. "You could meet the gang and have a good time."

Erin gave a wry smile. "Not this year," she said. "I'd like to see your dress though."

"I'll wear it up to the hospital and show it to you. It's different," she added mysteriously.

After lunch Erin went to the gym for dance class. It had been so long since she'd stretched and danced that she knew she'd be sore by the next day. Yet she was looking forward to the familiar muscle aches too. She put on her leotards and tights and was stretching when Ms. Thornton came in.

"Erin!" her instructor cried and embraced her. "I'm so glad you're back in school."

Erin quickly brought her up-to-date on Amy. Ms. Thornton shook her head. "I'm sorry she's not better. I went to Washington over the break to see my family, but I thought of you every day. I saw Allen, the director at Wolftrap, and mentioned your name. I told him how good I thought you were."

For a moment Erin's heart leapt; then it plummeted to her feet. "I haven't danced since the recital, Ms. Thornton. And I can't dance now. Not the way I'd need to in order to be in shape for an audition with Wolftrap."

Ms. Thornton touched Erin's arm. "Erin, you're a born dancer. You deserve the best training so that you can share your gift with the world."

Erin thought of Amy hooked to machines. She deserved to share her gift with the world too. "It's too much to think about now, Ms. Thornton. How can I even ask my parents about me going to Washington all summer?"

Ms. Thornton nodded. "I understand, but please don't give up the idea entirely. There's always next summer," she added.

"Sure," Erin agreed. "There's always next summer."

Ms. Thornton started to leave. "Oh, by the way, I have a cassette for you in my office of Amy's readings from the recital. I thought you'd like to have a copy."

For a moment Erin was overcome by her teacher's kindness. She cleared her throat, struggling to hold onto her emotions. "I'd like that very much. Thank you. I'll pick it up when I'm done here."

Later, when she did get the tape, Erin slipped into a bathroom stall because it was the only place she could be alone. She wept silently, holding the tape in her palm, remembering the terrible night when her world turned upside down.

Erin didn't know how long she stood there, shut in the stall, but she started when she heard voices. Two girls had entered the rest room.

"Don't be a drag, Cindy. Let's double-date. Spring Fling's more fun when you go with a group," one girl said.

"Fat chance," the other female voice countered. "It's taken me six months to get a date with Travis Sinclair, and I'm not about to share the evening with all of you."

At the mention of Travis's name, Erin pressed herself against the metal wall. What was the girl talking about? Maybe she'd misunderstood.

"How'd you ever talk him into going anyway? What with Amy still in the hospital and all."

"I just took a chance and asked him. I never really thought he'd come, but it was worth a try. I almost fell over when he said yes."

By now Erin could scarcely breathe. She felt hot and cold all over. Travis was going out with Cindy Pitzer. It was as obvious as if she'd seen Cindy on the other side of the door.

"Don't you feel bad about Amy?"

"Of course. But I don't know her that well, and I was dating Travis before she came on the scene anyway." There was a pause in the conversation; then Erin heard Cindy snap, "Don't look at me that way. It's just one crummy dance."

"But if it works out . . ." the second voice admonished.

"If it works out," Cindy interrupted, "then we'll double-date the next time. Now hurry up, or we'll be late for last period."

Erin stood in the bathroom stall long after Cindy and her friend had gone. She couldn't believe what she'd overheard. Travis was going out with another girl while Amy lay in a coma! She was so angry, her whole body shook. *Well you're not going to get away with it, Travis!* she vowed under her breath.

She let herself out, gathered her things, and left school, cutting her final class. All the way home she plotted revenge. She didn't know what she was going to do, but she would do something to get even with him. Travis would pay for treating her sister this way.

Erin skipped school on Friday and spent the day walking around the mall, moody and brooding. Travis's betrayal goaded her, and it wasn't just Amy he'd betrayed. She felt as if he'd betrayed her too. Hadn't he told her how much Amy meant to him? Hadn't he ignored Erin because he "cared" so much for Amy?

That evening at the hospital, she shared her day with Amy in a one-sided conversation. She never forgot what the nurse had said about comatose patients being able to hear, and she babbled on about the latest fashions and the newest makeup colors, feeling guilty about withholding the information about Travis and Cindy.

When the nurse came in to take Amy's vital signs, she told Erin, "Your parents are in the private consultation room, and they want you to meet them there."

Erin knew the room Laurie meant. It was a cubbyhole next to the waiting room, where doctors took the families of patients whenever they wanted to discuss something private, such as the results of surgery. Erin went to the room and let herself in. Her parents were talking in hushed tones to Dr. DuPree. Her mother looked as if she'd been crying. "What's wrong?" Erin asked, instantly alert.

"We've been waiting for you, Erin," her father said. His expression was grim, guarded. "Dr. DuPree was just going over the latest Glasgow test results."

"So what's the score?" Erin licked her lips. Her mouth had gone dry.

Dr. DuPree cleared his throat. "We've lowered Amy to a one-one-one."

Erin's stomach twisted into a knot. Suddenly she felt trapped and cornered. "Why are we in this room?"

"Your mother and I want you to talk to a man we met with earlier this evening," Mr. Bennett said. As if on cue the door opened and a man entered. He was tall and had black hair and a mustache. Erin's brows knitted together. She recognized him, but from where?

"Hi, Erin." The man thrust out his hand. "I'm Roger Fogerty."

Memory clicked into place. Neuro-ICU. A model

of a plastic brain. Words from a stranger with kind brown eyes. She'd asked, *"Are you a doctor?"* He'd answered, *"No. But I work with the staff here."* Erin took his hand, hesitant, wary. "Why are you here?"

His grip was firm and warm. His eyes caught and held hers hypnotically. "I'm with the Florida Organ and Tissue Donor Program."

Chapter Fourteen

Erin blinked, bewildered. Why would someone from the organ-donor program be here? Was one of Amy's major organs failing? Did they want to try some experimental transplantation technique on her? "I–I don't understand. . . ."

"This is always a difficult conversation for me to have with families, Erin. Would you like to sit down?"

"No."

Mr. Fogerty laid a briefcase on the table. Dr. DuPree stood beside him, and her parents sat rigidly in chairs on the other side of the table. Their shoulders were touching, but Erin thought they somehow looked miles apart. Mr. Fogerty snapped open the case and pulled out some papers. "I spoke with your parents earlier, Erin. Now I'd like to tell you about the donor program. About how the donation of organs can extend the lives of others. And about how some sort of meaning can be derived from your sister's tragedy."

"Donors are dead people."

"That's true, and—"

"Amy's not dead," Erin interrupted. "I've just come from her room."

Mr. Fogerty glanced quickly at the Bennetts. Dr.

DuPree came forward and leaned across the table. His voice was gentle as he told her, "Her pupils are fixed and dilated. The results of her EEG show that she's had no brain activity for about six hours."

Erin's gaze flew to her mother, who lifted a trembling chin. Erin took a step backward. Dr. DuPree continued. "We've run many tests, Erin. Blood-flow studies to the cerebral area, CAT scans—the newest, the best tests—and they all indicate that Amy is brain dead."

"Dr. DuPree has determined that there's absolutely no hope of recovery," Mr. Fogerty said very gently. "Now it's time to consider your alternatives. And donating Amy's organs is one of them."

Stupefied, Erin sputtered, "So that's what this is all about? You want to use her organs, and you need our permission?"

"The entire family has to be in agreement," Mr. Fogerty said.

Mrs. Bennett said, "You seemed pleased for your friend Beth's mother when she got news about her kidney transplant." Her face looked haggard and haunted, and Erin recalled how pretty her mother liked to keep herself.

"Th–that was different. The guy was already dead."

"Erin," her father spoke so quietly that she had to strain toward him. "So is Amy."

The room was silent. Erin heard the sound of her own blood rushing to her ears. "I don't believe you." But the look on her parents' faces took away her assurance. "I was just in her room, and I know she's alive."

"If we unhooked her from the ventilator, she'd stop breathing in minutes, and all her organs would begin to fail," the doctor said.

So that was the way it was, Erin thought. Amy was supposed to be dead, but without the machines her organs would be no good to them. She jutted her chin. "Well, I don't agree about donating her organs."

"Why?" her mother asked. "Shouldn't *something* positive come out of this hell? To help balance what's happened to Amy? Someone can't run out to buy sodas and just die! It makes no sense."

Erin felt as if she'd been slapped. *She* had let Amy go buy the sodas. Erin laced her fingers and cupped her hands demurely in front of her. "As long as the machines are doing their job, then maybe she can get better. But if you turn off the machines, then she'll die for sure."

"Haven't you heard a thing we've said, Erin?" Mrs. Bennett's voice sounded as tight as a wire. "Amy *is* dead."

Mr. Bennett silenced his wife and went to stand in front of Erin. "Baby, listen to me. Don't you think this is the hardest decision I've ever had to make? Kids are supposed to outlive their parents, not the other way around."

His face was contorted with pain, and Erin felt panic inside herself. She wanted to smooth it away for him. She wanted him to smooth it away for her. "It's not fair," she whispered through trembling lips.

"I agree," he said. "None of it's fair. And because I've seen so many unfair things in life, I've come to realize that while we can't expect fairness, we can expect mercy. And right now the merciful thing to do is to accept the results of the tests and turn off the machines."

The doctor took a step toward Erin. "Erin, please believe us. Technology is what's keeping your sister breathing." The lamp's light sent silver reflections off his hair. "You know, it used to be that doctors declared a man dead when he stopped breathing. And then we decided, 'No. He's not dead until his heart stops.' But we learned how to start hearts again, and we learned to build a machine to breathe for him. So we had to change the way we determine dead. Brain activity is our standard today."

"And donating organs is about the only good thing that can come out of something like Amy's death," Mr. Fogerty added.

Erin turned pleading eyes to her parents. "You can't let them do that. You just can't let them turn Amy off and then give her away in pieces."

"Stop it!" Mr. Bennett cried. "Is that what you think we're doing? I'd cut off my arm if I thought I could change what's happened to Amy. I'd donate any organ I had, if I thought it would save her. I'm her father, for God's sake. I gave her life. She's half of me." Tears glistened in his eyes.

Erin felt cold and numb, and a lump in her throat felt the size of an iceberg. She recalled a movie she'd seen in which a giant computer had become "human" and tried to take over, and after much combat had been turned off. Its lights went out one by one as it begged for another chance. What if Amy was like that? Dependent on the machines, crying to get out of the arena where she was trapped between life and death? "Labs make mistakes on tests," she said.

Dr. DuPree shook his head. "Not this time. I'm declaring her brain dead, Erin. And once death is de clared, and the family agrees to donate a victim's organs, we can't turn off the machines." His voice was tender and compassionate. "We must maintain her bodily functions if we're going to take her up to surgery and retrieve her organs for donor transplantation."

"Retrieve?" Erin said the word bitterly. "Is that what you call killing somebody so you can take their organs?"

"Erin!" her father said sharply. "That's uncalled for and not the point of this discussion at all."

By now Erin felt sick to her stomach and so icy cold that her teeth were chattering. "Why should I believe you? First you ask if you can put a 'Do not resuscitate' order on her chart, and now you want to 'retrieve' her organs. Why can't you just keep her alive until the great world of technology finds some way of making her better?"

"It doesn't work that way," Dr. DuPree told her. "Once brain death occurs, the body begins to deteriorate in spite of the machines. We have only a few days at the outside if her organs are going to be viable for transplantation."

"That's why I'm here, Erin," Mr. Fogerty explained. "I want to answer any questions you might have about organ donation."

She glared at him, suddenly furious at this stranger. "Well, I don't have any questions. You aren't going to cut up Amy."

"There's no disfigurement, Erin," Mr. Fogerty said. "She'll look the same as she does now."

"Is that why you were in ICU the night they brought Amy up? What do you do, Mr. Fogerty, hang around the halls waiting for someone to be declared brain dead so you can move in and take their organs?"

"Erin! Stop it!" Mrs. Bennett cried, rising to her feet. "They're just trying to help."

"I won't stop it," Erin yelled. "I won't, because I'm the only one who can keep them from taking Amy into surgery for dismantling." Her anger kept boiling, and all she wanted to do was hurt all of them.

Dr. DuPree and Mr. Fogerty didn't flinch. She hated them most of all. "I don't agree to 'organ retrieval,'" she said hotly, spitting the words like venom. "You'll have to find somebody else to give away."

Mr. Bennett sat back down heavily, reminding Erin of a balloon that had lost all of its air. "You're just upset. You don't know what you're saying." He looked to Dr. DuPree. "Give us some time together."

The men left, and Erin faced her parents. "Don't try to talk me out of it," she warned. "I'm not going to change my mind."

Her mother was crying openly. "Do you think we *want* to do this? For the love of heaven, Erin, just *think*! Amy's dead, and nothing's going to change that.

But we have the chance to make something good come from it." She fumbled in her purse for either a tissue or a cigarette.

"Leave her alone, Marian," her father interrupted on Erin's behalf. "It's too much for her right now. Just let her think about it."

Erin bit her lip until it bled. There was nothing to think about. She wouldn't change her mind. Her mother sagged down into the chair and buried her face in her hands, and her father put his arm around her shoulders. Erin felt left out and utterly alone. "I'm going home," she said. "And I'm going to bed. I'll come back up in the morning and check on my sister. Maybe something will have changed by then."

Erin left them. All the way home she silently warred with herself, her parents, the doctors. She couldn't believe that they were giving up. That they were turning Amy over to some faceless program that would take her apart and send her away to be placed inside somebody else. In spite of knowing Beth and how much it meant to her family to receive a new kidney, this was different. This involved her sister, and Erin didn't want to donate her organs like money to a charity. And deep down she clung to the hope that as long as she said no, some miracle might happen, and Amy would begin to rally—that all the tests would be wrong, and that Amy really was alive.

Inside her house she flipped on all the lights because the place seemed so empty, but even the blaze of lamps couldn't disperse the gloom.

Her mind felt numb. She thought about calling Shara but realized she couldn't talk about it. There was no one for her to turn to about this. Erin headed for her bedroom, got as far as Amy's door, and stopped. She reached out and grasped the knob, turned it, and stepped inside.

It didn't look like Amy's room. It was too neat and orderly, everything stacked and in its place. Slowly Erin walked around, visualizing it as it would be if Amy were home. "The bed would be unmade," she said aloud.

Erin pulled back the covers and tossed the pillows. "And there would be clothes all over." She went to the closet, tugged things off hangers, and heaped them onto the tumbled bedcovers. "And there'd be stuff sticking out of drawers," she said, pulling sweaters and lingerie so that they spilled out of the drawers.

"And Amy wouldn't approve of all these dumb papers in all these dumb stacks." She grabbed up a handful and flung them in the air and stood while they rained down on her like giant pieces of confetti.

"Her makeup would be all over the vanity table." Erin opened bottles of foundation and perfume and compacts of eye shadow and powder and blusher. She scattered some crumpled tissues and smeared one with Amy's favorite shade of lipstick.

Erin caught sight of the photos edging the mirror frame, Travis grinning out at her. She pulled the photo from its place and studied it. Memories from weeks before came back to her.

Amy asking her to work for her at the boutique. *"Pretty please. I'll be your best friend."*

Amy talking about the concert. *"I came up with an alternate plan. I told Travis you'd go with him."*

Amy at her birthday party saying, *"Life isn't fair,"* and *"I'll never be late again. Promise."*

"I hate you too, Travis," Erin told the photograph. She picked up Amy's eyeliner and drew a pointed beard on Travis's chin and horns coming out of his head. She wanted to tell him about Amy and what the doctors wanted to do with her. She wanted to see the expression on his face when she told him, "They say she's dead, and they'd like to cut out her heart and give it away. You know, for the good of humanity."

Suddenly she decided that that's exactly what she would do. Saturday night when he came home from taking Cindy to the dance, she'd be waiting for him. She'd tell him, and then she'd throw the teddy bear at him and suggest that maybe Cindy would like it for her collection. After all, how many people could say they owned a stuffed animal that once belonged to a brain-dead girl?

Chapter Fifteen

The next morning at the breakfast table, Erin and her parents sat in a strained and total silence. Erin assumed they hadn't seen Amy's room and was a little disappointed. She wanted a fight—they were all acting too polite and reserved to each other, and she guessed their strategy at once. *Leave Erin alone. Give her plenty of space. Sooner or later she'll come around.*

Erin sipped orange juice without tasting it and swore she wouldn't change her mind—ever.

"I'm going into the boutique for a while," Mrs. Bennett announced. "I've got to focus on something else."

"And I'm going by Briarwood," Mr. Bennett said. "I've got a hundred papers to grade, and since it's Saturday, there won't be any interruptions."

"I'm going up to the hospital." Erin's words were crisp and delivered like a dare.

"We'll go by tonight," her father said, clearing his throat and avoiding Erin's eyes. Erin left without even saying good-bye.

In Neuro-ICU the day shift greeted Erin as usual, but she sensed something different in their attitudes. They were nurses, and their profession was for the living, and Amy was, well, somewhere in between. Inside the cubicle where Amy lay, Becky was checking her vitals. Erin asked, "If she isn't alive, why do you bother?"

Becky removed the blood pressure cuff and hung it on the wall. "We want to maintain proper body temperature and keep her oxygenated."

"Why?" Erin asked sharply. She felt as if they were maintaining Amy for some scientific experiment.

Becky stared straight at her, and for a moment Erin thought she saw the nurse's eyes glistening. "She's a *person* to me, Erin. A human being who I know was loved because your family has shown their love every minute Amy's been in this room. I didn't know her, but I care about her."

Erin almost unraveled on the spot. Ever since the organ-donor possiblity was mentioned, she'd regarded the medical staff as enemies. She didn't trust them anymore. "I'll be back," she muttered, and fled out of the unit. In the hallway she collided with Shara.

"Whoa! Hey, Erin. I've been looking for you." Shara eyed her narrowly. "Are you okay?"

"Fine." Erin sniffed, clinging to Shara's arm. The appearance of her friend, wearing her familiar trench coat, seemed magical, and Erin realized just how badly she needed an ally. "It's been a rough night, that's all."

"Want to sit in the waiting room and tell me about it?"

They settled in the sunlit room, which was now

almost empty. Only emergency surgeries were performed on Saturday, so unless you were waiting for an extremely critical patient, there was no reason to hang around. Erin plucked at an armrest. "Th–they say Amy's . . ." Erin couldn't get the words out.

Shara touched her arm. "I know."

"How?"

"Rank has its privileges. My dad's on staff here, remember? He checks on Amy every day for me."

Erin dropped her head wearily against the back of the chair. Knowing that Shara had been checking on Amy's case all along comforted her. "So you know they want us to donate Amy's organs."

"Asking is SOP—standard operating procedure. There are plenty of people who need transplants, and not enough people donating their organs to go around."

"I think it's ghoulish. How can they ask such a thing? Especially when the tests might be wrong and Amy might suddenly start to improve. If they just give her enough time, I know she'll wake up from her coma."

Shara jammed her hands into the pockets of her trench coat and tugged it tighter. "You up for a little tour?" Shara asked.

"Tour of what?"

"Come with me. You'll see."

Curious, Erin tagged after Shara to the elevators, which they rode down to the fifth floor. When the doors opened, they stepped out into a corridor painted pink and blue with nursery pictures stenciled on the walls. "This way," Shara said.

They rounded a corner and faced long horizontal windows that looked into a room filled with row after row of Lucite bassinets of newborn babies. Nurses in gowns, gloves, and masks changed diapers, wrapped and rewrapped blankets, and juggled crying infants.

"Babies?" Erin asked, dumbfounded.

"Cute, huh? I used to come here a lot when I was growing up. Daddy seemed to always have to deliver a baby in the middle of the night, so Mom and I would come and have breakfast with him. He was always so busy that if we didn't meet him here, whole weeks would go by without us having a single meal together." Shara pressed her nose to the glass and pointed to one baby whose tiny face was puckered with a cry. In the next cart another slept, oblivious to the noise. "Anyway, while we waited for him, I'd stand here and watch the babies. They were like living dolls, and I always wished I could hold them."

Erin watched the infants with their eyes scrunched shut and their mouths shaped like rosebuds and their hands balled into doll-sized fists, until she felt a softening sensation inside her. "Bet it's loud in there."

"You need earplugs."

"Okay, you're right, Shara, they're cute. So what?"

"Let's go around the corner." Shara took her to another window, but the babies in this room were different from the others. They were wired to machines and monitors, some so small that they could fit inside a grown man's hand. Ventilator tubes snaking out of their mouths were held fast by crisscrosses of white tape. The walls of their chests rose and fell rapidly, little stocking hats covered hairless heads, and their skin was so thin that Erin could see their veins and count their ribs. "Neonatal-ICU," Shara explained.

"I–I've never seen anything so tiny," Erin whispered, mesmerized by the scraps of human life attached to tubes and wires.

"They're able to save more and more of the ones born prematurely," Shara said matter-of-factly. "It's a good thing," she added, "but I wonder, is it the right thing?"

"What d'you mean?"

"Dad and I talk about it a lot. He's delivered some babies who are so premature that there's no way they can make it. And if by some miracle they do, they're so physically or mentally damaged that their whole life is spent in an institution."

"But they're alive."

"That's true. Daddy says that a doctor takes an oath to heal and restore and to relieve suffering." Shara looked Erin in the eye. "At the very least he's to do no harm. But still, I wonder—just because medicine *can* do something, *should* it be done?"

Vaguely Erin caught on to what Shara was implying. "Medicine's created a monster, right? We have the means to heal, but not the wisdom. Is that what you're saying?"

"Something like that. What wisdom is there in

keeping a person alive above all other considerations? Why should doctors keep restarting someone's heart if he's never going to get well?"

Erin's own heart thudded. "Or why not turn off the machines on a person who—according to all the tests—is brain dead?" She spoke caustically, raising her shield of anger to protect herself from her best friend's words. "If this is a lesson in how I ought to okay the hospital's game plan for Amy—"

Shara grabbed Erin's arm. "No way. But I've seen my dad work and worry over babies like these when there's no hope for them. But because he's delivered them, he feels responsible for keeping them alive." She stared hard at one baby in a corner of the room whose legs and arms were no bigger around than the width of two adult fingers.

"Dad says that God made us to live with dignity. Instead, medicine and science get all caught up in the technicalities . . . in the heroic measures. We put all our efforts into keeping a person alive at any cost. It's as if winning the battle is more important than the person."

Erin mulled over Shara's words. She'd known Shara for years. They'd talked on the phone about a million silly things, but she'd never realized what her friend thought about things as serious as they were discussing now. She pressed her fingers into her eyelids and softly said, "Shara, I hear what you're saying. But I can't give up on my sister. I just can't!"

Shara sighed. "No one's saying you should give up as long as there's hope."

"But I can't give up my hope just because of some stupid tests. You said yourself that they make advancements and breakthroughs in medicine every day. Maybe there'll be one tomorrow that'll help Amy. If they take her now and remove her organs, then what hope will she have?"

Very gently Shara told her, "Erin, it's not going to work that way for Amy. There's no cavalry coming in medical breakthroughs to save her."

"Unexplained things happen every day. Something still could happen to bring her back."

"They can't keep her on machines much beyond tomorrow," Shara said. "I've asked my dad to explain what happens. Once brain activity ceases . . ." She left her sentence unfinished.

Unable to respond, Erin studied the infants connected to the equipment. She understood the medical consequences of Amy's condition: without brain activity, the body simply wasted away. She cleared her throat and pressed the palms of her hands against the glass. "Crazy, isn't it? *Their* brains are working fine. It's their bodies that are struggling."

Erin stepped away from the window and turned toward Shara. "Thanks, Shara. Thanks for bringing me here and thanks for being my friend. I–I'll think about everything you've said."

They stood together in an intimate silence. Finally Shara broke it. "Look, I've got to be going. The dance is tonight."

The dance. Travis dating Cindy. Erin forced a smile. "You have a good time." They started toward the elevators. "I thought you were going to show me your dress."

Shara glanced up and down the hall. "I'm wearing it under my coat."

"Let me see."

Shara opened the coat. She wore a cream-colored tuxedo, complete with ruffled white shirt, rhinestone buttons, and red satin cummerbund. "I told you it was different. Kenny's wearing a black one just like it. What d'ya think?"

Erin nodded her approval. "It's terrific."

"We're both wearing high-top sneakers, and I've got a silk top hat too."

Erin couldn't help feeling envious. How she wished her life had not grown so complicated and so sad. "You have a ball, and call and tell me all about it," she told Shara.

"I will." Shara hugged her. "I'll be home tomorrow if you need me to come up here."

Minutes later Erin drove aimlessly through the streets crowded with Saturday afternoon shopping traffic. She passed a baseball field where a Little League game was being played, and a mall where a radio station was doing a remote broadcast. How was it that the world could be going on in such an ordinary way?

Erin kept fighting back tears and wishing there was somebody she could go to. An image of her father floated into her memory. She saw herself as a small girl sitting with Amy on her dad's lap while he read them a book of fairy tales. How safe she'd felt then, intoxicated by the scent of his pipe tobacco and after-shave.

She glanced out the car window and got her bearings. She wasn't too far from Briarwood, and more than anything she wanted to be with her daddy. She wanted him to tell her that everything was going to be all right. That like Sleeping Beauty, Amy would wake up if the right prince came along.

Chapter Sixteen

Erin walked the halls of Briarwood slowly, touching the rows of lockers as she passed. The smell of chalk dust and white paste and old books saturated the air, and her heels made a forlorn echoing sound as she went.

She passed the trophy cases and paused to read the plaques and ribbons and trophy inscriptions. *All City Champs—Soccer, 1978, 1980, 1983. Best in State—Debate Team, 1973, 1981, 1985, 1986.*

So what? Erin thought. Where were those girls now who'd brought back the trophies? Did the winners ever think about the awards sitting preserved and polished behind a glass wall? Why did wood and brass endure while life evaporated into the wind? It didn't seem right.

She sighed and shook her head. The thoughts were too heavy and the questions too complex. An ache had begun between her temples. She hoped her dad had some aspirin in his desk.

Erin moved quickly until she spotted her dad's classroom, the eerie quiet unnerving her. She might have barreled headlong inside, but something made her stop short in the doorway. Maybe it was that sound—a sound she knew but couldn't quite place until she looked inside the room.

Her father was sitting at his desk, which was covered with papers, his arms resting on the wooden desktop and his face buried in the fabric of his jacket. He was weeping. Great, racking sobs were making his shoulders heave, and the sound he made was like that of a person whose soul was being torn away.

For a stunned moment Erin stood and watched. "*Real men don't cry. Is that it?*" he'd asked her the day they'd looked through the photo albums together. And she'd answered, "*Real men stick by the people they care about.*" Her heart pounded. *Oh Daddy. Poor Daddy*, she thought.

For a brief, panic-stricken moment, she didn't know what to do. She wanted to go to him and hold him, but she knew his tears were too private, too sacred for her to intrude upon. Erin flattened her back against the wall outside the door and shut her eyes, but the image of her father was burned into her mind forever.

Slowly she slid down the wall, biting her lip and resting her forehead on her knees. The tears came in quiet streams, and somehow she felt connected to her father by a cord of grief, as a spider's web connects two tree branches by its shimmering threads.

Erin parked her car on a side street near Travis's house and waited for him to return from the dance. She checked her watch. It was well past midnight.

"Cinderella's coach should have turned into a pumpkin by now," she said to herself.

While she waited, she carefully plotted her strategy. Travis lived in a fine old house on Bayshore Drive. When he pulled into his driveway, she'd call to him and make him cross to the bay side of the street, where she'd confront him. They'd be alone, and she'd say everything that was on her mind. He was a louse and a creep, and she'd make him pay for abandoning Amy.

When his headlights turned into the driveway, her mouth went dry, but the hard, cold knot of anger gave her the courage to call to him. Travis hesitated, so she called again, then watched as he jogged hesitantly across the deserted avenue.

"Erin?" he asked, coming closer. "What are you doing here?"

"I want to talk to you."

"Now? It's one o'clock in the morning. How long you been waiting?"

"Never mind. Did you have a good time at the dance?" Her question was laced with acid.

"Yeah." He drew the word out slowly. "Is that why you're here?"

"Of course. I just *had* to know if you and Cindy had fun at the dance. If you had a few laughs about old times and old girlfriends."

Erin knew that her barb had hit home. Travis glared at her. "Butt out, Erin. My life's none of your business. Don't you know? Life's short. We have to grab all the gusto—go for the gold. Know what I mean?" He turned, but she grabbed his arm. "Let go."

Years of dance training, coupled with anger, made her strong, and she tightened her grip. "I'm making it my business for my sister's sake."

"Has something happened to Amy?" His tone was wary.

"You mean you still remember her name? How interesting. I would have thought you'd forgotten it by now. You haven't been to see her in ages, have you?"

"I saw all I wanted to see that day in the hospital."

"And what did you see, Travis?"

"I saw Amy lying there like a vegetable." He broke her hold and started up the sidewalk that encircled the bay. Erin went after him. His strides were longer, but she kept pace. "I owe you nothing, Erin. Get out of my face."

"Well you owe Amy—you owe my sister plenty!"

He spun toward her, seizing her shoulders. His expression had become fierce. "I told you once that I'd never met anybody like Amy. She was wild and a little bit crazy, and we had a million laughs together. But when I walked into that hospital room, when I saw her lying on that bed with tubes and wires and hoses—" His voice quavered, and it surprised Erin. He dug his thumbs into her arms until it hurt. "*That* wasn't Amy. That was some shell."

"It *is* Amy," Erin insisted through clenched teeth.

"It's Amy's body, but it's not Amy's—" He searched for a word. "Where *is* Amy, Erin? Where's that special *thing* that made her Amy? That made her *real*. Tell me."

If her arms hadn't been pinned, Erin would have slugged him. She hated him. Hated him for asking a question she couldn't answer. She searched desperately for a way to hurt him. "Well, I think Amy's really up in that hospital trying to wake up. *If* they don't take her into surgery and remove her organs for medical science first."

Travis's grip loosened, and she saw his confusion. "What are you talking about?"

"You don't know, do you? If you'd been up to see her, you'd know that yesterday they declared her brain dead."

For an instant he looked as if he might be sick, and Erin stepped back, rubbing her arms and feeling confused. It was the reaction she'd wanted, wasn't it? Hadn't she come to hurt him? He said, "I–I didn't know."

"Well, with your big date with Cindy and all, I can see how it might have slipped by you." She reached inside her jacket and extracted the teddy bear. "Here's a little something I thought you'd like to have back," she said, holding the bear toward him. "Maybe Cindy would want it."

Travis knocked the bear from her hand, then turned and braced his hands on the cement railing. "You've got a mean mouth, Erin."

She wanted to leave him alone to think about how he'd wronged her sister, but her feet suddenly felt like lead weights. "I told them that they weren't going to cut up my sister and give her away. I said that I didn't care what their stupid tests showed, *I* wasn't giving up on my sister." She paused. "Like some people have."

"You think just 'cause I don't hang around Amy's bedside that I don't care? That I don't hurt?"

"You have a strange way of showing it, Travis."

"What am I? A robot?" His voice dropped, and Erin had to lean closer to catch all his words. "See, your problem is that everybody has to act exactly the same way for it to be legitimate with you."

"That's not true."

When he glanced up, she could have sworn that there were tears in his eyes. But he blinked, and then there was so much shadow that she couldn't be sure. "So you do penance by hovering over your sister and making sure everyone feels guilty for not caring the way you want them to."

"You're crazy."

"Am I? If they tell you she's dead, Erin, why can't you believe them? Let her go. For everybody's sake, let Amy go."

She shook her head vehemently. "Doctors have been wrong before."

"But what if they're not wrong?"

"You're not getting off that easily, Travis. I know what you're trying to do. You're trying to confuse me so you don't have to admit you're so disloyal to Amy that you're dating before she's—" She stopped the flood of words because she'd been cornered by them.

"Before what, Erin? Finish the sentence."

She started to tremble. Below her, waves continued to hit the seawall, and her head began to pound. "Drop dead," she told him.

"This is the way I deal with it, Erin. Cindy doesn't mean anything to me but I'm going on with the rest of my life because it helps me get through, because life is too short to waste."

Erin felt defeated. "I should have known telling you anything about Amy was a stupid thing to do."

"I can't change what's happened to Amy. And neither can you."

They stared at one another in the moonlight. The scent of jasmine mingled with the salty smell of the bay. Travis glanced up and down the sidewalk that wound along the water. "You know, I've suddenly got the urge to go for a run," he said. "At this hour you don't have to get out of the way for other joggers. Yeah, the world's pretty empty right now. And I'd never have figured that out if you hadn't come by tonight, Erin. So—uh—thanks for the tip."

Erin, silent, watched him run away. She had nothing left to say to Travis. He was a total stranger, and Erin wondered why she'd ever liked him, why she'd ever been jealous of Amy over him.

Erin picked up the stuffed bear and started to heave it out into the bay, but she stopped. The bear's glass eyes glittered in the streetlight. "You're such a mess, teddy bear," she said. "I'm sorry. You didn't do anything wrong."

Erin cuddled the bear and started to cry. As she stared at Travis's figure, now just a speck in the moonlight, his plea kept coming back to her. *"Let her go, Erin. For everybody's sake, let Amy go."*

Chapter Seventeen

"Erin, what are you doing here this late? Your parents left hours ago," Laurie, the night nurse, said when Erin stepped through the doors of Neuro-ICU.

"Yes, I know," Erin said. "I stopped by the house to get some things and told them that I was spending the rest of the night up here. I just want to stay with Amy." The clock on the wall read three A.M., and as Erin walked through the unit, she remembered how bizarre the machinery had seemed at first. Now her senses had become anesthetized to the blinking green lights and the rhythmic sounds she knew were sustaining life.

She stepped inside the glass-walled cubicle and set down her duffel bag at the foot of Amy's bed. "Hello, Amy," she said, squeezing her sister's hand and willing Amy to squeeze hers back.

"I'll bet you're wondering why I'm here," Erin said. "Okay, so you're not wondering, but I'll tell you anyway." The steady hiss of the ventilator was Amy's only response.

"I miss you. You probably never thought I'd say something like that. But the house is sort of empty without you." Erin felt her head begin to pound, and she pressed against her temples. "Oh by the way, I trashed your room. I know you would approve. I mean, if you could have seen how they cleaned it up—even the dust bunnies were gone."

Erin smoothed the sheet over Amy's chest. "And I need to tell you one other thing, Amy. I—uh—went to see Travis tonight. He had a date. It was with Cindy, but I don't think he had a very good time. We sort of argued about him dating and all. It made me so mad, Amy—I don't know how he could do that to you. But that's not really what I want to tell you about Travis." She took a deep breath. "You see, Amy, all these months—even before Christmas—I've sort of liked him. I mean, I *really* liked him. I thought I loved him." Erin's palms were sweating. Why was it so hard to get the words out? "Remember the night I went to the concert with him? I wanted to go *so* bad, and then when you sort of arranged it to happen . . . I couldn't believe it! But you know what? He never stopped talking about you the whole night. I guess I knew way back then that he never could have been *my* boyfriend."

Erin watched the ragged line of her sister's heart monitor. "I've thought a lot about it, Ames, and I realize that I didn't really love *Travis*. I just wanted to love *someone* and have somebody love me the way it is in books and movies. Maybe someday it will be that way for me, but it won't be with Travis. I hope you understand about me liking him behind your back." Amy's chest rose up and down in cadence with the ventilator.

"So, how will I tell you when my Mr. Right comes

along? How will I let you know if you're never gonna wake up?" Erin placed her palm along her sister's cheek. The skin felt dry and cool. Abruptly she stood and paced to the foot of the bed. "Look, Amy, I didn't mean to get all mushy on you. Forget all that junk about Mr. Right. I brought some stuff for you." She reached into the duffel bag and pulled out a book. "Remember this? Daddy used to read it to us when we were little."

"*Nursery Rhymes*." She read the title aloud. "Remember how we'd both sit on Daddy's lap and he would read to us? It used to get me mad because you always had a zillion dumb questions like 'Why did the man put his wife inside a pumpkin?' or 'How come she cut off the tails of the poor blind mice?'" Erin shut her eyes and tried to block out the images from her childhood. "Geez, Amy, we never had any of the answers. I'm sorry."

She switched on the light over the hospital bed. "Speaking of Daddy, he's taking all of this kind of hard. And I don't think Mom's doing so good either. They look older, Amy. I guess we all do."

Erin pulled a chair next to the bed and opened the book. She read a few of the nonsensical rhymes, until her eyelids got heavy and the words began to blur and run together. She realized she hadn't slept for two days.

"Let me borrow your pink sweater, Erin. Please? I'll be your best friend." Erin jerked awake. For a moment she was disoriented, then she spotted the book lying on the floor near her feet. She reached up and

flipped off the fluorescent light and listened to the steady rhythm of the ventilator. *In, out. In, out.* Across the room a child crouched bedside the machine wearing a flannel nightgown and holding a teddy bear. Her dark hair looked ruffled as if she had just woken up.

Erin shot out of the chair. Her heart raced as she stared hard into the shadows, but now she saw only the wall and a towel on the floor. She was hallucinating. Agitated, Erin fumbled with the light switch. "You ruined my pink sweater, you know. Oh you were sorry and all that, but it didn't take away the pizza stain on the front."

"Oh let me go! Please. I've had my license for a whole week, and I still haven't had a chance to use the car."

"How about if we go together?"

"I want to drive by myself this time. Pretty please? I'll be your best friend."

Erin felt herself growing angry as she spoke about the sweater. "You're so careless, Amy. Why can't you be more careful? Why can't you be more responsible?" Suddenly she felt foolish. Hadn't the doctors told her Amy was beyond hearing? Erin quelled her anger with a long sigh and took up her vigil in the bedside chair.

"I have something for us to listen to." Erin unzipped her duffel bag and fumbled for the cassette player. "Ms. Thornton gave me a tape of the dance recital, and I thought you'd like to hear your reading. You were pretty good. Even if you were always late for rehearsals and—" Erin stopped, because her fingers had encountered a sheaf of papers. She withdrew the packet, saw Amy's name, and remembered the day Miss Hutton had given them to her. At the time she'd shoved them into the bag and forgotten about them.

Erin put on the tape and leafed through Amy's old tests and quizzes and book reviews. The music from the recital sounded. Shara's voice sang and Amy's voice read:

> *"O Lord, thou has searched me and known me. . . . I will praise thee; for I am fearfully and wonderfully made. . . . Whither shall I go from thy spirit? or whither shall I flee from thy presence? Thine eyes have seen my unformed substance; and in thy book they were all written, the days that were ordained for me. . . ."*

Erin stopped listening to the tape and began reading one of the papers that Miss Hutton had given an A+.

> Subject: English
> Assignment: Essay
> Date: February 9
> Name: Amy Bennett
>
> *Sisters*
>
> *My very first memory is one of my sister's face. Erin was wearing a cardboard*

crown she'd gotten at a hamburger place, and she told me she was a princess and I was her maid. I had no reason to question her—princesses don't lie—so I served her tea and sneaked cookies from Mom's pantry, and when I was caught I took my licks. (Maids are always supposed to be loyal to their employer, especially when that person's a princess.)

Whenever she dressed up in her tutu and toe shoes, I thought my sister was the most beautiful girl in the world. And when she was six and went off to school without me, I sat by the window and cried all day long. She must have felt sorry for me because when she got home she told me, "School's not much fun. They make you line up just to go to the bathroom." Then the next year when I had *to go to school, I didn't want to!*

Erin and I shared a room until I was eight and my grandmother died. Then Erin got her own room, and I cried about that because I missed her. I also got all her hand-me-downs, her old toys and books, her case of the chicken pox, and all the valentines from the boys she didn't like in the third grade.

But she taught me stuff too. She taught me how to spit water through the space between my front teeth. She taught me how to get even with mean boys ("Don't hit them—shove them!"), and she taught me how to use makeup and how to put together neat outfits. She also taught me that you should never keep people waiting. (This is something I'm still working on, but at least I know *I should be on time, and someday I'm going to surprise her and never be late again.)*

Sometimes I hate being the "baby" of the family. It's awful being told "You're too young," and "Why can't you behave like your sister?" But Erin took up for me lots of times and once got punished for flushing Dad's pipe tobacco down the toilet (I wanted to see it swirl in the bowl and turn the water brown).

In two years Erin's going off to college, and it'll be a time of new freedom for me. No more sharing the bathroom. No more waiting for the vanilla ice cream to be eaten before we buy chocolate because vanilla's Erin's favorite. No more being fussed at because Erin's room's neat and mine's a mess. No more borrowing her *car,* her *hair spray, or* her *pantyhose. No more sister's shadow to live in. I'll miss her like crazy. (Of course, I can't tell her because I'd never live it down.)*

In summary, I believe that sisters are more than blood relatives. Over time they either become friends, or they wind up kill-

ing each other! Sisters are made by living every day with each other and wearing each other down until the rough spots are smooth. They're made by sharing secrets you'd never tell Mom, and out of doing things for each other just because you feel *like it, not because you have to. I guess you could say sisters are "grown," not manufactured, in a very special place called a family.*

Erin finished reading and let out a long, shuddering breath because it felt as if something heavy was pressing against her chest. She had never known—never even guessed—that Amy had felt that way about her. So many times Erin had simply brushed Amy aside, ignored her, or worse—teased and kidded her. Especially when they'd been younger. Now she saw that Amy had always cared about her . . . had loved her.

She brushed away moisture from her cheeks. *Grown, not manufactured*, Amy had written. *Fearfully and wonderfully made*, Amy's voice had said on the tape. Erin gazed at her sister's body. The eyelids were slightly parted, and she could just make out Amy's once-blue eyes, now glassy like doll's eyes. "Fixed and dilated," Dr. Dupree had said.

"Where are you, Amy?" Erin whispered. Through the years she'd asked, "Where's Amy?" a hundred times, but now the question took on a different meaning. Amy's body breathed, but it wasn't alive. Her heart beat, but it was a mechanical thing—

a pump. The essence of Amy—her soul, her will, her personality—was gone. All that was left was an illusion, a trick done with machines. The days that had been ordained for her had run out—for Amy time was over.

Erin felt a sense of resignation, of finality. She touched the tube protruding from Amy's mouth, fingering the tape that held it in place. Gently she rested her head on her sister's breast and listened to the heart beating strong and steady.

Erin shut her eyes, lost herself in the echo of false life and whispered, "Good-bye, Amy. I love you."

Chapter Eighteen

"Erin, are you absolutely sure you want to do this?" Mrs. Bennett asked over the conference table in the consultation room.

"I'm sure." Erin rubbed her eyes wearily, ignoring Dr. DuPree and Mr. Fogerty, and concentrated on her parents. In truth she was totally drained and exhausted. She was tired of fighting the inevitable.

"Once you sign the papers," Dr. DuPree said, "we'll gather the organ-retrieval team and take Amy upstairs for surgery."

"There are people who will benefit this very day from your generosity," Mr. Fogerty added.

Erin held up her hand. "Please, spare me the details."

"You don't really want to do this, do you, Erin?" her father asked.

"It doesn't matter anymore. Amy's dead. I believe that now, so what difference does it make if we donate her organs?"

"We have to be in agreement."

"I'm in agreement," she said dully. She watched her mother hunch over the table and scratch her signature on the bottom of the consent form. Mrs. Bennett slid the paper to her husband, who signed it too. Erin noticed that his hand was trembling.

Dr. DuPree took the paper. "Would you like to see your daughter one last time?"

"Yes," Mrs. Bennett said, and as Erin followed her parents to Neuro-ICU, she couldn't help thinking that this is how a condemned person must feel as he walks to his execution.

At the door of the cubicle, Mr. Bennett turned and said to the assembled staff, "My family and I want to thank you for all the care and support you gave us."

"We'll pack up her things and send them down to the Patient Consultant Office," Becky said. "That way you don't have to come back up here."

Erin saw that Becky had tears in her eyes. She wanted to reach out to her and say, "It's all right. You did everything you could. I'm not mad at you anymore." But she said nothing.

The three of them went into the cubicle where Amy lay. Erin walked to the opposite side of the bed from her parents, feeling strangely detached, as if she were standing outside herself and watching a movie.

"Good-bye, baby girl," Mrs. Bennett whispered. She didn't touch her daughter.

"Good-bye, Princess," Mr. Bennett said.

Erin said nothing, because she had already told Amy all she'd wanted to say. But she did want to touch her sister one last time while her skin was warm, while her heart still beat and her chest still moved with the flow of air into her lungs.

Erin stroked Amy's arm. She looked alive. She

felt alive. *An illusion*, she reminded herself. The fingers on Amy's hand twitched and flexed. "She moved! Amy moved," Erin said, incredulously.

Dr. DuPree rushed into the room. "It's spinal reflex," he said, patting her shoulder. "I assure you that's all it is, Erin."

"No! I saw her move."

"Erin, honey—" Mrs. Bennett said, her voice anguished. "I saw her move once too. Remember, I told you. But it wasn't real. Amy's dead, Erin. She's really dead. Please believe us."

The expression on everyone else's faces told Erin that her mother wasn't lying. She kept staring at Amy's hand, but there was no more movement, no more sign of life. "How can you be sure? How do you know?" she fired at the doctor.

"Because nothing else has changed. Her pupils are still fixed and dilated—"

"Stop it!" She was crying and couldn't stop. "Nothing's real around here! Everything's fake!"

"Perhaps a sedative—"

"No! I don't need one. I need to get out of this place. It's rotten. It stinks! Just go ahead and take Amy upstairs and get it over with. Do you hear me? Get the whole thing over with!"

Her father reached for her, but Erin backed away, found the door, and bolted. She ran down the hall, desperate to get away from the hospital. In the car her hands were shaking so badly, she could hardly get the key into the ignition, and once she did, she was crying so hard, she could barely see to drive.

Erin never remembered how she got home. She simply found herself parked in the driveway, and the next thing she knew she was in her bathroom. The odor of the hospital seemed to cling to her skin and clothes, making her gag. She wanted to be sick, but her stomach was too empty.

Erin felt dirty. Still crying, she stepped inside the shower and turned on the water full blast. Like fine needles the hot water stung her face and arms. She picked up the soap and ran it up her arms, across her blouse, and up her neck. If only she could get clean again.

She turned her face upward and let the water pour over her, trying to wash away the cloying smell of death that was strangling her.

Chapter Nineteen

The Bennetts kept Amy's funeral simple, choosing to have only a grave-side service for their family and a handful of friends. Erin would have liked for Beth Clark to be there, but she was still in Gainesville, where her mother was recovering from her transplant operation. Erin asked Ms. Thornton to come, and of course Shara, whom she asked to sing.

"What song would you like?" Shara had wanted to know.

"You choose," Erin told her. "Something special for Amy. Something for all of us."

Shara hugged her. "Oh, Erin, I'm sorry. So sorry."

"It's almost over," Erin told her. "Just one more day, and it will all be over."

The April morning of the burial smelled fresh with the promise of summer, and the vivid colors of the sky and grass made the day seem more like a garden party than a funeral. Wildflowers bloomed, butterflies danced, honeybees gathered pollen. Erin wondered how the world could look so beautiful, how creation could be so active on such a day of sadness.

Her parents had dressed in black. They both wore sunglasses, and her mother had bought a hat with a wide brim that flopped low over her forehead. Erin had decided to wear white. "It's the color the Japanese wear for mourning," she'd told her mother when she'd started to express disapproval. "Besides, I don't think Amy would have wanted everyone dressed in black. Too drab."

They sat together in a row, facing Amy's coffin, which was surrounded by baskets of flowers. During the service Shara leaned over to ask, "Are you all right?"

"Yes, I am," Erin told her. Her eyes were dry, and she meant it. "I guess I got everything out at the hospital. This part almost seems like an afterthought."

Erin tried to concentrate on the minister's words but kept getting distracted by the world that surrounded them. Somehow it seemed to her that all creation was dancing, and she began to sway slightly to the silent, secret music of clouds and sunlight, flowers and insects.

At the foot of her chair she spotted a dandelion. She plucked it, and inspecting it, realized how perfectly it was made. Its head was a symmetry of seeds that resembled stars, each connected to the central core. *Earth and sky*, Erin mused. She was holding a tiny universe in the palm of her hand! Trying to be inconspicuous, she raised the dandelion to her lips and blew gently; then she watched as the seeds scattered and sailed away.

The minister finished his eulogy, and Shara stood. Erin listened to her friend's voice but kept watching the dandelion fluff floating in the air.

"Amazing grace, how sweet the sound,
That saved a wretch like me.
I once was lost, but now I'm found,
Was blind, but now I see."

Was blind, but now I see. The words bounced around in Erin's mind like echoes off empty walls. She caught her breath in wonderment. Suddenly she *saw*, truly *saw*, something she hadn't seen before. Because of the gift of Amy's eyes, someone was able to see the beautiful world again. And because of the gift of Amy's heart, someone else was able to breathe the fresh, clean air for another day.

The flowers, the butterflies, the greening of the grass, told her that life was cyclic, season after season. It came, it went. It came again. And that just as the dandelion had shed its seeds to take root and grow again, Amy had given herself to all the tomorrows of someone else's life.

Erin gazed at Amy's coffin, draped with a mantle of pink roses, and knew with certainty that Amy wasn't in it. Maybe her body would be buried, but the person of Amy, her spirit, would not. For Amy was with Erin still and would live in her heart for all the days of her life.

Around her, chairs rattled, and with a start Erin realized that the funeral service was over. Her father reached out and took her hand. "We made it, honey."

"Yes, we made it."

Her mother leaned against her husband and he

cradled her to him. He slipped his other arm around Erin. "I'll bet Amy would have liked the service," Mrs. Bennett said.

"She would have liked it," Erin agreed.

Her parents started for the long black limo parked on a narrow roadway, but Erin lingered behind. Shara stood next to her, sniffing back tears. "Your song was perfect," Erin told her.

"Thanks. I was afraid my voice would break up." Shara eyed her. "I know this is an awful day for you Erin, but you look . . . well, settled. Sort of peaceful."

Erin lifted her face toward the sun. White clouds billowed overhead. "I feel peaceful."

Shara said, "I always envied you, Erin, because I always wanted a sister."

Shara's confession surprised Erin. Seeing fresh tears pool in her friend's eyes made Erin want to comfort her. "Sisters are special, and they have something very special between them." Erin smiled mysteriously. "But you know, Amy and I were much more than sisters—we were best friends."

If you enjoyed reading *Somewhere Between Life and Death,* be sure not to miss the companion novel, *Time to Let Go*.

"Did you drive your car today?" Erin asked Shara.

"No, Dad dropped me off on his way to make hospital rounds. What's wrong, Erin? Another headache?"

Erin never tried to keep the headaches a secret from her friend. Her parents had asked Shara's father, Dr. Perez, for the names of doctors to treat her when the headaches had first started. "It came on real sudden," she said.

"You want me to drive you home in your car?"

"Could you, please?"

Shara quickly gathered up their things. "Do you have your pills with you? Maybe you should take some."

"Yes, you're right." Pain stymied her. Why hadn't she thought of that? She found the pills, took two without water and leaned against the lockers. Her breath was shallow. "I wish it didn't hurt so bad."

"Your doctors still haven't found what's causing them?"

"Not yet." By now Erin was feeling sick to her stomach. She gripped Shara's hand and allowed her friend to lead her out of the gym. Outside the late afternoon light stabbed at her eyeballs like hot needles.

"This isn't right, Erin," Shara muttered. "You can't go on this way. How are you ever going to do the play?"

Erin dug her nails into the blond girl's palm. "*Please*, don't say a word to Ms. Thornton, Shara, okay? Not one word."

"You know I won't. But I can't stand to see you hurting like this."

Erin thought she heard Shara's voice catch. "I want that part, Shara. And I'm not going to let these stupid headaches stop me." She was dizzy now and very nauseous. She braced herself on the car while Shara fumbled with the key.

"Even if you have to play opposite David Devlin?" Shara asked shakily.

Erin tried to nod, but every movement sent fresh waves of agony shooting through her head. "Even that," she whispered falling across the seat as the door opened.

Erin made it home, where she took her headache medication and crawled into bed. Nausea made her gag and she writhed on the cool sheets praying for the pain to go away. But everytime she closed her eyes, the image of David Devlin replayed in her mind.

She didn't know why. She couldn't explain it. Yet she was completely and absolutely convinced that somehow David Devlin was mixed up in the headache's arrival.

About the Author

Lurlene McDaniel has been a professional writer for more than twenty years and has written radio and television scripts, promotional and advertising copy, and a magazine column. She began writing inspirational novels about life-altering situations for children and young adults after one of her sons was diagnosed with juvenile diabetes. She lives in Chattanooga, Tennesses.

Lurlene McDaniel's popular Bantam Starfire books include *Goodbye Doesn't Mean Forever,* the companion novel to *Too Young to Die, Somewhere Between Life and Death, Time to Let Go,* and *Now I Lay Me Down to Sleep.*

Lurlene McDaniel loves to hear from her fans. You can write to her % Bantam Books, 1540 Broadway, New York, New York 10036. If you would like a response, please include a self-addressed stamped envelope.